EVERYTHING I DID GOOD:
WAS ALL BAD 2

By: Jonathan Fox

CHAPTER ONE

My stay at Oak Hill youth detention, turned out not to be so bad, once everyone found out I could fight, and wasn't scared to do so. I spent a lot of time in the gym, working out, and just kicking it with homies I knew from the streets. Nikki had been writing me faithfully, sending me money orders, and pictures.

I wrote back always thanking her, but I never led her to believe I was coming home to be with her. At first, I told her not to send me her money, cause she needed it for her baby, but that just seemed to make her send more money. Plus, that loot started to come in handy. After my six months was up, I bid farewell to the boys and the alliances I'd made. I felt happy and sad at the same time. I knew there were always chances of coming back so, I left on good terms with everybody. Like a true gentleman and gangsta would.

Back on the bricks, "Whew!" the smell of fresh air, the vibrant colors, the feel of fresh street clothes. I was so exhilarated, I couldn't wait to see my buddies. I got home, and it was the same depressing atmosphere. My buddies were floating around in the neighborhood somewhere.

There was no red carpet rolled out for me the way I expected. I had imagined coming home and everybody setting shit out for me and giving me gifts, happy to see me, but it wasn't anything like that. As I was walking down the street towards my building, my nigga Dinky pulled up in a blue old school Impala with a burgundy top with silver Daytons rims.

"Aye Squirrel!" He yelled.

I turned and automatically patted my hip. I forgot I had just come home and didn't have no weapon, old habits were hard to break.

"Damn Dinky." I said looking at him in awe. "That joint sweet Youngin'. I heard while I was in, you were doing the damn thing." I walked towards his car.

"Nigga get in." He said.

I got in and the interior was plush, Dinky, was a light brown-skinned young hustler out the neighborhood, who was fly as shit. He was getting money. He had two brothers, his oldest brother was a big-time hustler named, Little Feet Kevin, and his younger brother's, name was Boo-Boo.

All them niggas were out there hustling getting money and they all dressed fly. Dinky was more on my level though. He was cool and would fire his hamma with no problem.

"Nigga since you been gone, we all been jive on the come up. Omar, got him a Taurus Wagon. Ronald, got a police package."

A police package was an old police car that was of no use to the police anymore, so they sold them at auctions for the low.

"Ya man Black Mike, got a sweet ass Cadillac, 81 Fleetwood, Midnight blue, with tints, and one hundred spokes. That joint the truth, Joe. Tye got a white LTD with Duallys on it. Lil' Anthony got a 280 Z. Greg, couldn't save his money. He was hustling, but he spent his money on money hungry females. He was a sucka for love, every time we'd look for him, he'd be in his house shacked up with some freak, trying to hide her.lol Oh yeah, and man the police towed your shit! We saw it sitting in six D's parking lot. We broke in it and took out your clothes, coat, and system. I got yo' shit at my house, I'll bring it to you later." Dinky said.

"Man, I'm glad you home Young." A dude named Sandman been looking for you heavy. Slim getting it too, he'll be back through, he come every week. I'ma take you shopping joe." Dinky continued. He reached in his pocket.

"Here you go, Young." Dinky handed me five hundred dollars.

"I appreciate this man." I told him, I was so grateful. "Ain't got nobody else looking out for me." That was real big of him.

"Look don't go nowhere, Young. I'll be back to pick you up. We gonna go get you straight my nigga." He smiled. "I just gotta make a run over 21st Street, me and Wordy, gotta holla at some folks. I'ma see you later." He stopped the car in front of my building.

"Young, I'll see you later." I said, giving Dinky a hug, and some dap. I was happy as hell, when I exited the car.

Dinky had lifted my spirits, there were some good men still left.

****

That day I waited and waited. *'Damn where Dinky ass at?'* I thought.

As I waited for Dinky, a couple dudes stopped by and showed me love. Mike, Omar, Tye, Ronald, Lil' Anthony, Greg, Boo-Boo, Antwon, Black Frankie, Rashard, Light-skinned Mike, and more. Only Black Mike, Light-skinned Mike, and Tyran crazy asses gave me money.

I wasn't trippin', I was happy just to be back in the hood, seeing these niggas. Big Doris had found my stash of money and spent it. When I came in the house and saw that I was through. I asked her about the money, she claimed she needed it.

"Damn all that money?" I asked.

"Yeah muthafucka, you should've been giving me some…"

I blocked her out, I'd already accepted that loss. I was broke now, I had only two thousand dollars to my name.

Where the fuck is Dinky? I thought again. "Fuck it." I grumbled, then went in my room and went to sleep.

The next morning when I came outside, it was empty. I walked around the hood and everywhere I walked niggas was looking sad. As I started back towards my house, Dinky's brother, Little Feet Kevin called me.

"Hey Squirrel!" He yelled.

I turned back around. "What's up, Kevin?" I asked, walking back towards him.

He looked sad. "Man, Dinky called me before he and Wordy, left yesterday. He said y'all was supposed to go shopping for you."

"Yeah." I said. "Dinky never came back to get me, Joe. He gave me five hundred dollars and bounced. Where Young at anyway?"

"Squirrel Dinky in the hospital on life support." Kevin replied sadly.

"What...what the fuck happened to my man, Joe?" I was shocked. "Man, I'ma crush some 'em." I was pissed.

"Nah, Joe calm your ass down." Kevin said. "Dinky and Wordy, was in a car accident around 21st Street yesterday.

He was turning at the light when a speeding car came balling smack into the driver side. Wordy flew out the window, but he alright. Dinky got smashed up."

Tears flooded my eyes, "Damn, that's why my man didn't come back."

"He's at Howard University Hospital in intensive care. Right now, he can't have visitors. I don't think he gonna survive, and if he does the doctors said it's a ninety-five percent chance, he gonna be a vegetable." Kevin started crying. "Man, I know he wanted to take you shopping bad, that's all he talked about. We had a surprise for him, for his birthday coming up.

"I'ma honor his last wish. The last thing he said was he wanted to get you a lot of fly clothes. Here's the keys to his grey Malibu Station Wagon. We faked liked it was stolen, that's why he bought the new Impala, so, we could fill it with clothes and gifts for his birthday.

"Everything in it is brand new. We bought him all brand new clothes. All of its yours now. After you clean the car out, I want you to burn it. Squirrel, I won't be able to stand seeing my brother's car driven around here and him not being in it." Kevin admitted.

"I understand, Joe, thanks Kevin." I replied.

"No problem…I know you and Dinky was tight. He was always talking about you. I know he fucks with you from the heart. Just honor my wish." He said.

"I got you, Joe." I promised, as I stepped off.

"Oh yeah welcome home, Youngin'!" Kevin called out.

I wanted to see what gifts was in Dinky's car. I went around the building to a long alley. I walked down to the place, Kevin told me the car would be. I saw it at the end of the alley. As I approached the station wagon, I saw balloons that had *'Happy Birthday'* on them and a lot of boxes. I used the keys and opened the door. I felt Dinky's presence already, when I opened the boxes there were brand new colognes, clothes, socks, shoes, boots, jeans, two black leather jackets, and four Polo sweatshirts. Me and Dinky wore the same size shoes and clothes luckily.

I was happy as hell, but sad for my man. I knew he couldn't do anything with all this shit though. I took it home, drove the car around for a minute to sight see, then burnt it on Kelly Millers field. I honored Lil' Feet Kevin's request.

CHAPTER TWO

Before I burned Dinky's car, I drove around Good Hope Road, Southeast to see my aunt. I knew her, my uncle, and cousins would be glad to see me. As I parked and got out of the car, I saw my cousin Little Shrimp. I walked up to the porch, as he ran towards me and gave me a hug.

"Squirrel!" He squealed excited.

"What's up, lil' man?" I said. "Where's the fam?"

"In the house." He answered.

Shrimp a.k.a Teddy was my cousin Ada's son, but he lived with my aunt Tinan and Uncle Bobby-Lee. He was really short to be nine years old and smart as a whip. He knew things that you wouldn't expect a kid his age to know, but he was very sneaky.

Over the years all three of my female cousins had moved out and had children. I continued to walk up the steps into my aunt's house. As I walked in the door, everybody greeted me with open arms.

"Heyyy Babby!" Aunt Tinan said.

I spoke and hugged her, shook my uncles hand, gave Li-Poo, dap and an embrace, then sat at the dining room table.

"I gots to cook you something to eat boy. I know you hungry." Aunt Tinan, commented. In her country accent.

Indeed, I was, Aunt Tinan went into the kitchen and yelled back out. "I need some flour and seasoning salt. Squirrel, I'ma need you to run to the sto' fo' me at the corner. Just let me get my purse."

"Nah, Aunt Tinan, I got it!" I yelled back.

"What?" She asked.

"Nah, I'll pay for it." I repeated, as I got up, and headed for the door. "Anything else you need." I asked before leaving.

"Nah baby."

"Alright, I'll be back."

I stepped out of the house and walked to the corner store.

"Excuse me ma'am." I said to the chubby female cashier. "Where's your flour and seasoning salt?"

"Aisle three for the flour, and right over there for the seasoning salt," she said flirtatiously.

I playfully winked at her. "Well, thank ya' ma'ammm!" I said in my best southern accent.

She busted out laughing. I went, got the items, and came back to her register. She was smiling from ear to ear. She was about to ask me my name when...I heard someone call me.

"Fox."

I turned around and saw the most beautiful green eyes staring at me. I immediately knew who she was. It was green eyed Keisha from school.

"Boy, what you doing around here?" she asked.

"Girl, I get around." I replied.

"And where have you been? School has been boring without you."

"Well I been in a little unfortunate situation." I shrugged.

"Keisha, who him?" A very pretty, silky haired, pecan skinned, 5'5, curious eyed, older woman asked.

'Daammnn!' I thought.

"Oooo...ooo...oooo...Peaches this the boy Fox, I was telling you about. The one that saved me from the asthma attack and looked out for me. The one that can fight really good. He goes to my school." Keisha was talking quickly, jumping up and down, excited.

I felt myself blush like a kid, for the first time in my life. I had no idea she talked about me that much.

"Fox, this is my Aunt Peaches." Keisha introduced us.

"*Aunt*...she fine as a muthafucka." I told myself, and she carried herself more like a young lady.

"Nice to finally meet you, Fox." Peaches said.

"Nice to meet you too, Peaches." She was staring directly in my eyes. "Well nice seeing you, Keisha. I hope y'all enjoy your day." As I started to walk pass.

Keisha grabbed the arm of my jacket sleeve. "Boy, I can't get no hug or nothing before you roll. Damn I ain't seen you in like forever." She said smiling.

Shit, this was a new Keisha, she was bold and beautiful. Usually she was quiet and cute. I put the bag on the counter and gave her a hug.

"Good God." I hadn't been embraced by a female in a minute. Standing there with her in my arms felt so right.

Her voluptuous titties, pressed against my firm chest, and she hugged me tight. After the hug my private area was bone hard.

"Here you go, call me." She wrote her number down.

I grabbed the pen, wrote down my new pager number and handed it to her.

"You better call me too." She threatened jokingly.

I looked at Peaches, she smiled at me behind Keisha's back. A smile like a cat who'd cornered her prey. I grabbed the bag off the counter and walked back to my aunt's house. Once my aunt finished cooking. I ate and told them stories about how I ended up at Oak Hill and how it went once I got there and so forth.

****

A week later, I was in the hood. I had on an Gortex Red pullover jacket, and some blue jeans, with a pair of butter double soled Timberlands.

I had blown most of my money. I was down to two hundred dollars. I hadn't even thought about flipping some yay or getting another car.

Everybody else was had their money in order. I decided fuck that I'm about to get back on the feet, catching the bus wasn't cool. I wanted to go see my cousin Barbra. She had moved from 10th Place, Southeast to Ridge Road, Southeast and see how she was doing. I caught up with my man Tubby, who had also just come home from Lorton.

"Aye Tubbs." I hollered.

"What's up, Squirrel?" He said. "Let me borrow your car. I'ma make a run around Ridge Road to see my cousin." I said.

"A'ight hold up!" Tubby answered.

Tubb, was a tall dark-skinned hustler around Lincoln Heights , who lived three buildings over from my building. He was one of the original mazed hustlers, but he had got locked up for an armed robbery and done a bid.

Now he was home and back on the grind. Tubb came back talking on his cell phone, as he threw me the keys to his sky-blue LTD.

Tubb also had a green Corvette, he rarely drove. Niggas was out here getting that bread. I walked to the car, got in, started it, and drove off. I had been thinking about Green eyed Keisha. Somehow, I had lost her number.

'Fuck it, I'll see her in school.' I thought. But damn I had to get re-enrolled. I reached Ridge Road and parked on top of the hill. As I got out of the car, I felt stares from everywhere.

I patted my hip. "Aww shit, I forgot my hamma. Damn I'm slipping." I mumbled.

I reached the door to my cousin's apartment and knocked.

"Who is it?" she yelled.

"It's Squirrel!" I yelled back.

I heard Barbra unlock the door and snatch it open. "What's up nigga?" She shrieked with joy, hugging me.

"Ain't shit." I said. "I just came through to holla at you."

Barbra's boyfriend *Conk* came out of the bedroom. "What's up, Young?" He spoke.

"Ain't nothing just getting home." I said.

Conk was a short cocky dude, with nappy thick hair, he'd been on edge with the men in our family, because he used to beat on Barbra. The only reason I hadn't killed him, was because of my cousin. After all, the fights they'd gone through, I could see she really loved the dude. I kept my peace, he didn't know, I knew the drop on him and every hang out spot.

I'd followed him many times. I had to stay one up, in case I decided to kill him one day.

Barbra played Go-Go music and danced. We talked all that evening, until it was time for me to take my man Tubb's car back. I promised, I'd be back to visit often because we had a good time, laughing and listening to music.

As I was coming down the stairs from her apartment there were a group of dudes hanging on the steps.

"Shit, I gotta walk through these, bamas." I grumbled under my breath, as I continued down the steps. "Excuse me fellas," I said.

Some of them politely moved out of the way. A couple of them stayed where they were, so I'd have to step over them. All of them had on army fatigues, with black T-shirts, or jackets.

I knew this part of Ridge Road, was beefing with 37th Place, across the street from them. I wish I was carrying my pistol,at that very moment. This was drama all the way live. I could tell they were all carrying firearms. I knew Barbra was standing in the window waiting to see me come out of the hallway.

I yelled back upstairs on purpose. "A'ight cuz, give aunt Tinan and Uncle Bobby-Lee, my love!"

"Okay cuz!" She hollered back.

That was just to let these dudes know that I wasn't an intruder scoping their territory.

As I stepped down there was no use saying excuse me again, I'd said it loud enough the first time. I casually stepped over the dude and kept walking towards the front door.

"What tha…nigga what the fuck you think you doing!" A tall dark-skinned, skinny dude jumped up, and when I looked he had a gun in his hand. An all-black .9mm. I turned around to face him and my first thought was to always remain calm..

When I faced him, and got a full view of his face, we recognized each other.

"Lil' Fox!" The dude said. "Boy I was about to pet your pockets,slim."

It was a dude named Mike-Mike, his grandmother lived across the street, from my mother, and he had an aunt that lived in our circle in the hood. He was putting his work in for some big hustlers I knew, but word on the street was that he was getting too big headed and careless. He wasn't respecting the game, I noticed it from his quick temper and the way he carelessly pulled out his gun.

The advantage I had on him, was that he knew my brother Snuk would kill him in a heartbeat, but he didn't know I'd kill him quicker. Not today, though, today I was just gonna kill him with kindness. I could tell he had something on his chest. He wanted to challenge me bad.

"Damn Mike-Mike, what you doing around here, Joe?" I asked.

"My people live around back, Young! I be up here smoking and shit, just chilling." He said.

Another mistake he'd just made, letting me know where his people stayed and that he be up here high on that Love Boat…a.k.a PCP.

'Yeah, this bama is careless.' I thought. If I had to make him an enemy.

"Yeah, I heard you been n the come up Lil' Fox. Word spreads fast." He commented.

I felt the animosity in his voice. "Come on Mike-Mike, don't have me do that to you." I silently thought.

"But don't bring that drama up here, Joe." Mike-Mike continued.

Yeah, he had hate in his blood I'd never come this way again without my weapon. Just in case I had to protect myself up here. The dudes in the hallway smirked, knowing they had me trapped if it jumped off. I gracefully bowed out.

"Nah, Joe you got me mixed up." I replied.

"Nah, I know who's who, Lil' Fox." He retorted.

Amongst the circle of up and coming killers, they'd allowed this nigga to hear too much, now he was so big headed that he wasn't seeing any other respectable names in the game.

"I'm chilling, Joe." I said again. "See you later." I told him, as I stepped out of the front door.

As I came through the front door, I saw a group of girls standing in the front of the next building. I kept stepping thinking about the nigga Mike-Mike.

"Aye Fox!" I heard a girl holla.

I turned to see Green eyed Kiesha and black Yolanda, running up to me. I peeped the niggas in the hallway looking as well.

"Boy you sure get around." Keisha said.

'Damn it must be my lucky day. I didn't get killed and there I stood with this beautiful ass girl.

"Yeah I do." I replied.

"Are you following me, I live right here." Keisha pointed to the second-floor window on the right-hand side.

"My cousin lives in that building on the third floor." I pointed.

"Barbra your cousin?" Yolanda asked.

"Yeah." I nodded.

"Damn boy! Barbra, cool as shit!" Both girls agreed.

"So, what's up wit' ya?" Yolanda asked, seductively.

"Bitch you late, I got his digits already!" Keisha said smiling.

"Whaat, it's like that?" Yolanda questioned.

"Yeah, it is." Keisha said, grabbing my hand. "Come on Fox, let me introduce you to my mother." She led me by the hand, through the crowd of girls upstairs to her apartment.

One of the girls' teased. "Damn bitch, she just get her meat and run, just like a cave bitch!" All the girls burst out laughing.

When we were in her apartment it was dark as hell. The only light on was the kitchen, but it was small and somewhat cozy.

"Can I use your phone?" I asked her, so I could call Tubb's, because I had to take back his car.

Keisha said hold up and left out, she came back with a telephone on a long ass cord. She was using the neighbor's telephone. I realized, she didn't have a telephone. I called Tubb and asked him did he need his car.

"Nah, not right now, go ahead and keep that joint until tomorrow. I'll be up early." He replied.

"A'ight, thanks Tubb." I said as I hung up.

Keisha took the phone back next door and came back to the apartment. She grabbed my hand and took me to the back room to meet her mother. Once we were back there it was dark as well. Her mother was sitting on the bed with her boyfriend.

Keisha's mother was brown-skinned and looked nothing like Peaches.

"Ma, this my friend Fox, I told you about. The one from school that helped me." Keisha introduced.

When her mother turned to me, I could see her wild looking eyes. I knew that look.

"My name Louise, baby. Thank you for helping my baby. You're a real gentleman."

"Thank you, ma'am." I said.

"Oooh…you got respect and manners. I like him, Keisha." Louise squealed.

I could already tell she had sized me up. Louise was a crack head, I could smell the crack in her skin. She was high along with the boyfriend, whose name was, Lawrence. He was tall, with a big round head, and greenish-gray eyes. The joker looked crazy as a homeless man. I picked up on all the signs. I knew what was up, but I didn't speak on it. I played like it was normal.

Me and Keisha, went and sat on the couch in the living room. She cut on WPGC 95.5. We talked and talked, she told me she had a little brother, who was a year younger than her, a little sister named Raven, and another little brother named Man-Man, who also had green eyes.

All of them spent the night wit' Peaches. She was the only one that came home. The radio started playing the quiet storm. As the slow jams played, me and Keisha talked. I felt so relieved to talk to someone again. My pain was diminished, she threw all her troubles on the table and we comforted each other.

Before I knew it, it was four o-clock in the morning. Damn time had flown, it had been three in the afternoon, when I entered Keisha's apartment.

"Pretty eyes, I got to go home." I told Keisha.

She looked sad. I looked up and I don't know how my head ended up on her lap, she was playing with my hair. Even though, I was so comfortable laying on her soft thighs. I got up and headed for the door.

"Plus, I don't want your boyfriend, catching me coming from your house this time of the morning. I don't want to come between y'all." I yawned.

"I respect relationships, it's a beautiful thing. What about you?" She asked.

I had already told her about Nikki, betraying me and that was my first serious girlfriend.

"Well, when she comes along, I'ma hug and kiss her." I said playfully.

Keisha wrapped her arms around me tightly, as I hugged her back. Then she kissed me on my lips. Her lips were soft and succulent.

"Did you find her yet?" Keisha asked. "Because I believe she just found you and she wants to be your second and only serious relationship." Keisha admitted, continuing to j@ me.

I was stunned. "Wha…what about your boyfriend?" I asked.

"You ain't gotta worry about him. Him and I been over, it just took me some time to find you. I been had myeyes on you,,you just be faking. But you do have a good heart. And I wanted it, I promise to keep it safe, and protected." Keisha said.

She kissed me again and asked. "When will I see you again?"

"I don't know. I got some things to handle. Just call me." I responded, then kissed her on her forehead, and left.

CHAPTER THREE

"Squirrel…Squirrel."

I looked up in the cut, it was Tye calling me. He had on a yellow T-shirt, some black jeans, with some all-white Nikes, and this crazy looking hat.

"What's up, Young?" I hollered back.

"Hold up, I'm coming down." Tye jumped down the steps and came running towards me.

"Young, this dude came round' earlier looking for you. I forgot his name, he said he'd be back through. He driving a blue Maximum." Tye informed. "Young we missed the shit outta you. The hood was bored. Squirrel, I know you go-hard, but slim you went extra hard. Penny ass did the moonwalk when that fire got to popping." Tye laughed.

"Nigga it was all because of your crazy ass." I reminded Tye laughing.

"Man, we going down Virginia Beach to hear Essence and Junkyard play this week. You rolling?" Tye asked.

"Nah, Joe I'm broke. I'm sitting here thinking how I'ma get some more bread. I might have to put them hammas to use." I replied.

"Well you know I'm down for whatever, Young."

Tye was always with anything that had to do with getting money. He wasn't no fighter or shooter, but he damn sure 'nough was a con artist, hustler, and shit starting, funny muthafucka. You got some buddies that you can't even be mad at, Tye was the type, that just made your day. You can be feeling bad and he'd do something silly to cheer you up, he was forever scheming. I love his crazy ass.

"Aye Squirrel, you know Junk new tape out. They played it at the Ibex. That joint cranking, too." Tye said.

Tye knew I was a hardcore Junkyard fan. "Shit you know who got them tapes?" I asked.

"Maybe the bama on Minnesota Ave, you know it be a lot of tape sellers down there. Let's walk down there." Tye replied.

I thought about it, I was about to go get my hamma, but it be too many police down there. It's a good distance too.

"Let's go Joe." I told Tye.

As we walked, me and Tye kicked it about getting some money. He told me, he'd been flipping wholesales, plus he'd been boosting electronics and clothes. We used to do that back in the day, it was still in effect. Niggas had to eat and I was about to get back cruddy. It ain't no joke being broke.

We reached Minnesota Ave and walked straight to the vending tables. Every table we went to didn't have the newly released Junkyard tape performance at the Ibex. There was one more stand set-up with tapes, CDs, clothes, and more in front of the Giant grocery store.

We headed towards it, once we got there, it looked like the biggest vendor in the area. He had a mini- store outside, and a grey Ford van parked behind him blasting that new Junkyard tape we were looking for.

Once we were sure that was it playing, I tapped Tye so he could walk ahead of me, and act like we weren't together. This was our routine when we were about to scheme. Me and Tye never paid for tapes. We always stole them for a five-finger discount.

Tye walked ahead of me and pretended to be examining which tape he wanted to buy. Tye flashed a bank roll of bills, so the bootlegger was happy to accommodate him.

I waited for a while, then walked up slowly. When I reached the vendor stand, I immediately recognized the bootlegger. He was the same dude from a year ago who told me to *'Get the fuck outta here'!* He didn't know I had stolen five tapes that day. He still had a light beard, brown-skin, and was wearing a black skully.

He didn't recognize me once I walked up. I had grown since then. I peeped and saw his grey van sliding door was opened. Inside there were video tapes, cassette tapes, CDs, the Big LL Cool J radio blasting the Go-Go music, and plenty more.

"Damn if only a nigga could get that van." I said to myself.

I peeped at Tye, he was slyly looking at me, with a twinkle in his eyes. I knew he was thinking the same thing I was thinking. How were we going to get it with this nigga standing right here? As my thoughts roamed, Tye bumped my leg in front of the table, and flashed a flathead screwdriver he'd been carrying in his back pocket.

Tye always carried some tool, he used for multi-purposes. He was always prepared for a situation. I already knew he had plans on stealing the van, but how? Tye always had something up his sleeve, so I decided to go along with it.

Tye started browsing, acting like he didn't want the tapes.

"Man, you gonna buy some of 'em or not? If not step off, I got other business to attend to!" The vendor yelled at Tye.

This muthafucka, still had a smart-ass mouth. Tye faked like he was fed up and stepped off towards the Payless. When I saw Tye bend the corner, I knew he was gonna come around the back of the parking lot.

"Whatcha got champ on the Go-Go tip?" I asked, stepping up to the vendor, playing my role.

"Youngin' I got it all, Junkyard, Rare Essence, Northeast, Superior Groovers, Backyard. You name it, I got it, right here." He pointed at the table. "And that's, that new Junkyard band you hear in the back." He pointed his thumb backwards. "What you see is what you get." He replied.

I peeped Tye easing through the cars. "Man, which band you fuck wit' the most?" I asked distracting him.

"Well, I personally fuck wit' Rare Essence. They're more old school. I used to stay at Club Triples go-going. Especially, when Funk was on the lead, mic.

This joker went on and on. I rarely had to do much talking. He was so caught up, reminiscing, he didn't notice Tye had slipped into his van and was busting the steering collar. The blasting music suffocated the cracking noises of the screwdriver, breaking up the hard plastic around the collar.

The entire time this bama was talking. I was cuffing all type of merchandise right in his face. Suddenly the van door slammed shut.

'Goddamn, Tye works fast.' I thought.

That broke the bootleggers trance, the music was instantly muffled. He stared straight at me, I smiled, then it hit him. He'd just been winged.

"Remember me?" I asked politely.

He wasn't trying to hear what I was asking. He quickly turned and was unsure whether to run after his van or watch me. He knew if he ran over to his van, I was going to rape his table.

Damn sure nuff he hauled ass over to his van. The way he ran was as if his life depended on it. I grabbed the cloth that all the tapes and merchandise was on and began quickly wrapping the items into a ball.

"Aye...aye...get the fuck outta my van!" The bootlegger yelled.

I looked up from tying the knot, I'd tied in the cloth. Tye had all the doors locked smiling at the bootlegger. He looked over at me and saw that I had all of the vendor belongings tied up in the cloth.

"Man, don't do this to me!" He pleaded.

"Nigga, fuck you!" I yelled as I ran to the end of the corner with the cloth of merchandise.

As soon as I was a good distance away. Tye put the van in gear and drove over the sidewalk into the street. The bootlegger tried to hold the door handle, he lasted about four seconds until the van jumped over the curb. He flew off the handle, I busted out laughing, as he rolled like he was on fire.

Car horns were honking because of Tye's insane, rude driving. The bootlegger bounced a few times, then bounced back up to his feet. That seemed to wipe the grin off my face. Now this nigga was running full speed at me.

"Oooh...shit, Tye come on nigga." I hollered.

Tye was just clearing the traffic, I picked the sack up, and ran further down. The guy was gaining and shortening the distance between us. The van pulled up, Tye got out of the driver's seat and slide the side door open. I threw the sack of merchandise in. The Go-Go music was still blasting. Tye jumped back in the driver's seat, I hopped in and looked back.

"Go...go...go!" I screamed at Tye.

The bootlegger was closer than I thought. I slammed the van door and heard a *THUNK*. He had crashed into the side door, from running so fast.

The traffic cleared just in time, Tye peeled out into the traffic and drove back to the hood.

"Damn nigga that was close." I said.

****

Me and Tye made it back to the hood. I told Tye to park the van in the alley, where Dinky's car was once parked. As we parked in the vacant alley. I slid the side door open to see what we came off with. I had cut the boom box off, that was mine.

"God dizzamn. We came up wit' the come up!" Tye said.

It was boxes of all kinds of merchandise. It reminded me of when we were burglarizing houses. We emptied every damn box and split everything down the middle. As we were leaving the van with our merchandise, the thought hit me that it might be some money in that bitch. We didn't do a thorough shake down of the joint.

"Hold on, Tye." I said.

"Where you going, Young? Let's get this shit up and roll." Tye said.

"Man, we didn't shake this joint down thoroughly." I told him.

I went back to the now empty van and slid the side door open. I looked around, then started searching the seats.

"Squirrel, I'ma run this shit up to the house. I'll be back to get yours, this shit heavy." Tye hollered.

"A'ight Joe." I yelled. "I'ma be right here."

Tye started walking up the alley, with the sacs of shit. I was searching so hard, I was sweating. I searched every part I could think of when a thought came to me. I jumped up and down on the van floor. I pulled the heavy mats up and just like I thought there was a square box in the floor with a little lock on it.

The hidden spot was so neat, you would never be able to tell the stash was there. I remembered seeing a crowbar in the back where the spare tire was. I went back there, grabbed the crowbar, and came back. I pried the little lock off and opened the latch.

"Bingo, cash muthafuckin' money! That's why the bootlegger was running for this muthafucka like his life depended on it." I saw the stack of hundreds, fifties, and twenties.

I reached in, pulled out the money, and guess the ount to be around twenty bands. It was seventeen thousand, nine hundred, ninety-two dollars.

"Ooowee!" I yelled.

I was about to exit the van, when I thought of one more spot. I climbed in the driver's seat and just observed the dashboard. I went in the back and grabbed the crowbar, went back up front, and pushed the seats all the way back. I stuck the crowbar in the seam of the dashboard and pulled backwards. The whole dashboard snapped off and I fell back on my ass.

When I looked, I was right again, another stash. There was a black metal box and a .380 pistol. The metal box was heavy as a muthafucka. I shook it, and heard what sounded like coins, it had a big lock on it.

"I'll get this shit open in the house." I said to myself.

I looked up and saw Tye walking back down the alley. I reached in my pocket and counted four thousand dollars off the knot of money I'd found.

Man, I should keep all this shit! I thought. "Nah I'ma give my man something. I ain't no cruddy nigga."

When Tye approached I handed him the money. "Here you go, Joe. I found some money and I broke you off."

Tye's eyes got big as flying saucers. He counted the money. "Four G's! Man, we came up Squirrel." He said excited.

"Yeah and look." I showed Tye the gun.

"Damn, Joe, that shit sweet." Tye said. "You always follow your instincts."

Tye was so happy, he didn't even question me about how much money I'd found or what was in the big black heavy box I was carrying. I was all right with him not questioning me, too. We picked up the rest of the items and headed out of the alley.

CHAPTER FOUR

After boosting all of the merchandise and finding all that loot. I went and bought me two midnight blue and grey Brougham 89' Cadillac from Sheriff's Road Car Dealership in northeast Washington D.C. I was in the hood selling black market videos like hot cakes.

Tye kept his share, I sold mine like a true hustler. I sold every item I got from the bootlegger. The Metal black box I found was filled with quarters, dimes, and nickels, about five thousand dollars' worth. I kept that hidden in my room, I was back grinding again. Things were looking good.

I had five percent limo tints installed on my Cadillac windows, with one hundred chromes spoke fifteen-inch wheels. This caddy was clean as a new born baby and fast as hell. I had a big V8 in that joint.

I drove to see Keisha a couple of times, her and I had a good time. Our relationship was progressing. I was feeling shorty, things were still heated in my house, I needed her company. I'd drive over her house, as soon as I came in she would ask me.

"Are you hungry?" Then she would go into the kitchen and fix me something to eat.

'Damn I'm falling in love.' I thought.

Keisha would tell me come lay my head on her lap, so she could play in my hair. That shit always put me to sleep, Keisha seemed to have the magic touch.

Snuk had gotten locked up for possession of a gun out in Maryland. I'd also found out, he had a body, which is a murder charge. He didn't get caught with the murder weapon, but two eye-witnesses identified him as the shooter, a month earlier.

Snuk always carried hammas, but this murder situation brought something new into the game. I figured I'd set up some bond money for him just in case but the courts wouldn't give him a bond because of the murder.

Snuk had been getting himself together. He'd met a new girl from Simple City, named Tesa. They had, had a baby girl named Ta'wa, she was so beautiful. I used to baby sit her when Snuk got locked up the first time in D.C. for another gun possession.

Snuk had brought two apartments, one in D.C. and one out in Maryland for safety purposes. He was trying hard to be a man and be there for his new-found family, but the broad Tesa had other plans.

She was a hardcore party-goer and she had another baby father, who she was still fucking on the side and who was extremely jealous of Snuk. There'd been many occasions, I caught Tesa in the Go-Go talking and dirty dancing wit' other niggas. I used to tell Snuk, the broad was no good. But when Snuk falls in Love, Snuk's in love.

There had been many times me and Snuk had gotten into fights over her. I missed my brother, I felt she was doing him wrong. I told Snuk, I was going to kill her. He knew I was dead serious. Snuk begged me not to harm her for the sake of his daughter. I came to grips and honored his wish, but I was hurt and mad because this broad was a sneaky bitch.

What happened with the murder, Snuk had allegedly committed, was a mystery. He didn't go into details all he knew was that he had two witnesses testifying against him in Upper Marlboro Maryland.

"What's up lil' bro?" Snuk asked.

He'd been able to make a call from the jail.

"Ain't nothing." I responded.

"I'm facing a whole lot of time. You know Maryland don't play." He said.

"Man, how did you get caught for the jizzoint?" I asked.

"Maann… me and Tesa was having an argument and I left out. When I came back this stupid bitch called the Police. She said somebody else heard us and called the police. I believed her cause she knew not to do some hot shit like that, with all the demo I got in the spot. Somebody else had to call them folks.

I came back in the building and as I was walking up the stairs I heard police up there. So, when I turned to leave, two police were walking in the building, so I was trapped.

"I tried to play it cool and walk pass them, but they must have had a description and was looking for me. One officer asked me my name. I gave him an alias, Billy.

They were about to let me roll until one officer from upstairs peeped over the railing and asked them to search me for an I.D. I ain't know what to do, I couldn't run, plus they had me blocked off. I knew I was caught, so I submitted to the search. When the police felt the bulge in my waist he asked what was it?

"I tried to break free, but the other officer clipped me up and wrestled me to the ground. They arrested me and after I got to the station, that's when they threw the body at me. Somebody had told them I was the one who slumped a nigga in a parking lot down the street."

Snuk had gotten caught up on a humble. "So, what dey gonna do?" I asked.

"If the witnesses don't come, I'm straight. They just gonna fine me for carrying an unlicensed pistol. The hamma I had was clean, it didn't show up, so I'm good wit' that." Snuk replied.

"Damn maan." I groaned.

"Hey, can you kiss my peeps?" Snuk asked.

I knew that was code for making his witnesses did ape are. "Yeah, I'll give all my love to them." I responded. "Send me Ms. Birdie's address."

That was code for do you know where they live.

"A'ight I can do that. Oh yeah, I heard about your new green eyed pretty girlfriend, Squirrel. You've been spending a lot of time over her house." Snuk said.

Man, how the fuck did he know about Kesha?

"I know you wondering how I know about her, that is of no importance, just remember when you not watching your own back, I am. You my lil' brother and I love you." Snuk replied.

"If something happened to you, I don't know what I'd do. That's why I stay on your back so much. I didn't want you to turn out the way, I did. I admit you've done good so far, but there is always room to fuck up. Never get Big headed and never be so anxious. That will be your destruction. I know many secrets about you, but all secrets ain't for all men. I hold back to get you ahead, boy!" Snuk was telling me.

I just laid back and soaked up the game he was spitting. Snuk was always sharp in mind. I always respected his ditty-bop. He was a quiet, smooth, behind the scenes type of individual, and very dangerous.

"Hey, look stay around, you'll be getting a visit sometime this week…a'ight." Snuk told me. "Love you man!"

"I love you too!" I said as we hung up.

Damn now I got to sit around the house and wait. I always wanted to be out. I didn't want to deal with the drama inside this house. *'Being disciplined is everything!'* Snuk's voice came into my thoughts.

****

"Baby, where the fuck you been? I need to see you!" Keisha's voice hollered through the phone.

"I'm at home, Love." I answered.

"Fox, I miss you boo, come over here. What's wrong, are you sick? Fuck dat' I'm coming over there." Kesha was bombarding me with questions.

"Nah, I'm a'ight, I just been chilling girl. I had to stay around the house and help my momma." I replied.

"Well...can you bring your ass over here to see your girl?" Kesha asked.

"Yeah when I finish." I said.

"Fox, I know goddamn well you ain't been helping your momma for six damn days!" Keisha yelled.

"Hold up love, pump your brakes wit' your mouth piece. I done told you, I'm helping my mother. Don't start lunching out on me, girl." I said. Kesha was quiet, "You hear me girl?" I asked.

"Yeah, I hear you, but I ain't seen you, I miss you boy. So, if you don't come over here in a day or so. I'm coming over there and there better not be no bitch over there. I swear I'ma…"

"Look Keisha." I snapped cutting her off. "You the only girl I love, there ain't no other bitch…that's gonna steal my heart."

"Who you calling a bitch?" She hollered.

"Girl look…" a knock came at the door. "Hold up, Keisha." I said.

Before I got off the couch, I pushed the mute button on the phone. It had been six days since I'd seen Keisha. I missed her company, but this mission came first.

"Who is it?" I yelled out.

"It's Greg, Joe." I opened the door, "Hey Squirrel some dude out front looking for you. I told him to wait down on the side of the building." Greg said.

"A'ight here I come, tell him to hold on." I told Greg.

Greg went to deliver my message. I closed my door, "Hello…love?" I said.

"Yeah I'm here." Keisha answered.

"Look baby I'ma call you back."

"Your ass better call me straight back too." Keisha threatened. "And I meant what the fuck I said about you coming over here, if not expect me at your doorstep."

"I got you girl, I gotta go, see ya later." I told her as i rushed off the phone.

"Love ya." She said.

Damn green eyes was mean wit' it. She didn't know, that aggressiveness turned a nigga on. I grabbed my Glock .40, and stepped outside. I looked both ways because even though, I'd been gone. I didn't forget what Mohammad did to me.

His time was coming after I got myself situated. I walked to the curb and looked down the street. I saw a man standing there in a grey business suit with a briefcase.

A black BMW 735i was parked a couple of steps away from him. He looked totally out of place with that suit on, especially in this neighborhood. I nodded towards his car, he took cue, and headed towards it. I liked his style, once I got to his car, he opened the passenger side door. I had my .40 in my shirt sleeve in case this went wrong.

"I'm here on behalf of Mr. Fox." He said.

"Yeah, what's your name?" I asked.

"Did I ask you yours?" He retorted.

"Nah." I replied.

"Okay then we know each other on a no name basis." He said.

I respected that, it was some gangsta shit. I started getting excited, he handed me a piece of paper.

"Have a nice day." He said ending our meeting.

I got out of the car and he drove off real neat and smooth. This was some real shit, I couldn't believe how smooth he'd handled that.

Once I looked at the paper it had two names and two addresses on it. One was in Oxford Knoll Maryland and one was in Oxon Hill Maryland. Then it hit me, my brother said stick around someone would be by to visit me. This dude said he was here on behalf of Mr. Fox. They were the witnesses addresses.

"Think nigga." I told myself. "Stop acting like a lil' boy." I chastised.

Snuk's trial started in another three weeks, it was time to put my game face on.

CHAPTER FIVE

I went and stole me an old Caprice for the mission. I drove to the Oxford Knoll address first because it was the furthest. Damn, I realized I hadn't called Keisha. I knew I had a vicious tongue lashing coming.

'Fuck it, I had to handle this business first'. I thought.

I arrived at the housing complex, I knew this area a little because some folks I knew lived out there. I parked the Caprice two blocks down and got out. I had on an all-black Khaki jumpsuit. It looked like I was a maintenance man. I had two pistols on me. I also had a tool belt wrapped around my waist trying to disquisition myself just in case I got stopped or observed by some nosy ass neighbors. I'd look like a man coming home from work. My heart was beating fast as a muthafucka. Every time I was about to go put some work in my adrenaline went into overdrive.

I was looking for building 223 in Knoll court, I found it in the second court. Now I was looking for apartment 11, it was on the left-hand side. The house lights were on and I saw what looked like a woman in the kitchen.

"Goddamn, I can't do this shit." I told myself.

I was looking for a man named, Moe it was either now or never. I walked up to the building door.

"Just my fucking luck." I grumbled under my breath. It was locked. "I'm leaving."

As soon as I started walking away a young teenager said, "Excuse me, sir you forgot your keys, huh? I always do that, come on let me let you in."

I couldn't believe this crazy shit, I really didn't want to go through wit' it, but here was my chance. The youngin', was in a parked car smoking weed by himself. I slipped again because I looked around at the cars, but I didn't see nobody.

He must have had the seat leaned all the way back. He put his key in the door and let me in. I acted like I smelled weed, which I did. It was in his clothes, he hid his face, and hurried on, to the first court. He probably thought I was going to report him or something. My move worked just like I expected.

The people out there show a lot of hospitality. They grew up different from us in that city. When I was sure he was gone, I peeped the area and closed the door. The building had brick walls and it was quiet.

I went to apartment 12 and put a strip of black tape over the peep hole. This wasn't going to be a pretty sight. I listened to the door and heard a television. I slid the Ruger P-89 out and put on my ski mask. I knocked on the door and waited.

"Who is it?" I heard a child's voice ask. Then the door opened.

I immediately rushed in, I grabbed the little girl, and covered her mouth so she couldn't scream. The living room was empty. I peeped around the corner in the kitchen it was also empty.

I took her in the breeze way and whispered in her ear. "Where is Moe?"

"He…he…he in the room." Her little voice trembled.

"Who all is in the house right now?" I whispered.

"Just me, my…my…mommy and Moe-Moe." She was scared.

That must have been the woman I saw through the window. The apartment was big and plush. They had a big screen T.V., a Kenwood stereo system, black leather couches, and white and black carpet.

"Nee-Nee, who was that baby?" A woman's voice came from the room.

The little girl I was holding name was Nee-Nee. She looked like a little button. She was adorable, I would hate to have to kill her.

"That's my mommy." She whispered.

"Look tell her it was nobody if you don't I'ma hurt you and your mommy." I threatened. Then I uncovered her mouth.

"Noobody!" She hollered.

"Okay sweetheart." Her mother said.

"Good girl." I told her.

I looked into her eyes and for the second time I felt guilty. She looked so innocent. I looked around the kitchen and saw a microwave. I went in the drawers and found the biggest knife I could.

I snatched the cord out of the socket, grabbed Nee-Nee, and put her little head between my legs, while I cut the microwave cord. I heard her gasping for breath, I realized I was choking her. I lighten the pressure up between my legs. I didn't want to hurt her. After I cut the cord, I tied little Nee-Nee's hands behind her back quick and tight. Then I took her socks off, balled them up, and stuffed them in her little mouth.

I bent down, "You a'ight princess?"

She nodded, then lightly kicked my leg. I turned around, she was trying to tell me something. I didn't know if it was a trick, so I showed her the butcher knife to scare her. Nee-Nee's little eyes grew big as she understood what I meant. I took the socks out of her mouth.

"Please don't hurt my mommy mister, she loves me. I know you here for Moe not my mommy." She cried softly.

I stuck the sock back in her mouth and slid her body under the kitchen table. I pulled the table cloth all the way down. I was wondering where the fuck was her mother. I'm glad she or Moe didn't come out that bedroom. I peeped around the corner, I realized I hadn't put my gloves on so, I hurriedly wiped my prints off the knife handle, then slid my black leather gloves on. I peeped around the corner and looked towards the bedroom.

One of the bedroom doors was closed. *'Bingo, that's where they're at'?* I thought.

I crept through the apartment and looked into the bathroom, the door was wide opened to my left. The bedroom door that was closed was to the right directly in front of the bathroom. I listened to the door

"Oooh...baby...aahh...baby!" These muthafuckas were fucking.

That's why they had the baby out in the living room watching a movie. I opened the door, a dark-skinned, muscular dude, had a light-skinned female's legs thrown over his shoulders and was pounding her ass. She had her hands on the back of the headboard, while he was digging in her pussy.

"Moe!" I said.

That scared the shit out of this nigga. He screamed like a bitch and jumped ten feet in the air out of her pussy.

"Man, who you?" He yelled. "Girl you been cheating on me?" Now he was furious.

"No Moe!" The light-skinned woman cried.

"Bitch turn around before you lose your life." I yelled.

She looked confused until I pulled the Ruger out. She started crying and complied. She knew what it was, but if she stayed like that I wouldn't kill her.

"Man, we ain't got no money." Moe said. "You can have my watch." Moe bent down, and I shot him in the back of his neck.

The broad screamed.

"Shut the fuck up bitch, you ain't dead yet." I snapped.

I smelled their sex all through the room. And I couldn't Berlin ever ai was becoming aroused, and just seeing the sweat roll off her pretty, round naked ass, as she laid there on her stomach, had me tempted to fuck her, but that wasn't my style.

I'd never raped a woman, no matter how bad the situation was. I always thought if you rape a woman, you might as well kill her, because apart of her will be dead forever.

I walked over to Moe's limp body and pumped two more bullets into his head. The broad muffled a scream in the pillows. Blood was rapidly pouring from Moe's head.

The first shot came out through his esophagus. I walked to the other side of the bed, the broad was trembling like an earthquake. The aroma of her sex had me feeling some type o f way in my boxers. I bent down and inhaled her fragrance.

After a good sniff, I whispered in her ear. "Baby doll, I am not going to harm you. I'ma spare your life. Little Nee-Nee's safe, I know you're worried about her. And it's because of her that you're alive sweetheart. Your baby asked me not to hurt her mommy." I said.

The woman began sobbing uncontrollably. "Th...th...thank you sir." She mumbled still face down.

"No thank little Nee-Nee."

As I was about to leave I saw the phone, I went over pulled out my pocket razor, and cut the cord. I went all through the apartment. There were only two phones in the entire apartment. I tied her hands behind her back, then went in the kitchen. I lifted the table cloth, Little Nee-Nee was still under there, crying.

"Your mommy's not hurt."

Little Nee-Nee nodded her head, then I left. I exited the building real smooth. I had taken my gloves and mask off, and now I had a screwdriver in my hand acting like I'd just finished working. I looked at my watch, it was 12:49 a.m. I wanted to go home, but it was time to go to my next mission. As soon as I got a block away I heard police sirens.

"Shit!" I started a light jog to the Caprice, I hopped in, started it with the screwdriver, and drove off calmly.

Once I got on the highway I knew I was safe.

CHAPTER SIX

I pulled off Suitland Highway, into a gas station. I pulled over to the telephone and called my man Tree. Tree was my partna outside of the hood, we met when I was at Oak Hill. Tree lived out in Maryland but hung in D.C. on the southside. He had family all over D.C.

"Hello?" Tree answered.

"One-o-three click." I replied.

That was our code, one-o-three was a gang of hardcore niggas. Something like a secret society. Tree knew the code was urgent.

"I'm at G-station off Suitland Highway."

"A'ight." Tree said and hung up.

Tree knew Maryland like the back of his hand. Moments later a sky blue old school 78 Bonneville pulled in with tints and razor low profile wheels. The car cruised over to where I was standing, then the passenger window rolled down.

Ice Cube's song *'A Bird In the Hands'*, was blasting through the car speakers. That joint was off *Ice Cube's 'Death Certificate'* tape. I loved that joint.

"Get in, Joe." Tree said. I got in the passenger seat. "What da deal Young?" Tree asked, puffing on a fat blunt. "You wanna hit this?"

"Nah I'm in mode." I declined.

"Understood...understood." Tree nodded.

Tree had dreads in his hair, that's why they called him Tree. His hair looked like tree branches. Tree was medium height, brown-skinned, an always calm and cool dude. That was my nigga to the end, we ride or die together.

He was the only nigga I knew who was so calm and maintain his composure in any situation,besides Snuk. Tree was a thinker and I always respected his way of handling things.

"Man, I need to get around your way." I told Tree. "I got some business to take care of."

"Address?" Tree inquired.

"Yeah seven fifteen west Oxon Hill." I told him.

"Okay let's ride." Tree said.

Oxon Hill was his area, he and one-o-three click had that spot-on lock. I didn't know my way around there as good as Tree did.

"You see that house beside the corner house?" He pointed, once we reached Oxon Street on the backs streets.

"Yeah." I nodded.

"That's you right dere." He told me. "You toatin'?" He asked.

Tree lifted his shirt to show me a massive, smoke, grey P-90 Ruger .45 Caliber. I showed him the two P-89 nines, we both laughed.

"I just need you to make sure nobody run away from the house." I said.

"Gotcha!" Tree agreed.

The street Tree chose was dark, and it was damn near 2:50 a.m.

"Lil' Fox hey you see that other street over there?" Tree pointed.

"Yeah." I answered.

If you got to run, go through there, and follow the curve. It will lead you to my car. It's a stolen green Pontiac, two cars up. Start it and get ghost.

Damn, he was already a step ahead of me. That's what I liked about Tree, he was always expecting the unexpected.

Even though this was a residential neighborhood plenty of niggas sold drugs in the area. It would fool an outsider because of the nice looking houses, neatly cut manicured lawns, and decent up to date parked cars. Thankfully seven fifteen was a small house, because I didn't want to run through no big house. I'd have to smash everything moving. I looked around to make sure there was nobody in sight.

Even though I didn't see anybody, that didn't mean there wasn't somebody watching, the streets were always watching, so I had to make this quick. I went around back and pulled myself up to the window seal, so I could take a peak. To my surprise somebody was up watching T.V.

I jumped down quietly, I'd learned how to maneuver during my time as a burglar. I went to the other windows, I couldn't see through them.

"Okay." I breathed. "Here we go."

I went to the front door and knocked. I looked back and saw Tree squatting behind a brown mini-van. I pulled my lock pliers off the tool belt, I still had wrapped around my waist.

"Who is it?" a half feminine-masculine voice called out.

"Scuse me ma'am my car broke down. Can I use your phone please?" I asked.

The door opened and there was a woman with long light brown hair, dressed in mini shorts, she had sexy long legs, and some fluffy slippers on her feet. Her toenails were painted red, she had on a little T-shirt which showed a hairy stomach.

Her face was soft and delicate with what looked like long thick fake eyelashes. She blinked bashfully flirting with me.

"Uumm...um...um...um, yes you may use my phone anytime darling." She said. "Um and you're a handy man? I might need a tune up myself." She flirted.

I smiled, "I'm sorry am I disturbing your family?" I questioned.

"Oh, heavens no honey, the only one here is me and my boyfriend. He's sleep, his ass drunk, a bitch can't even get no dick." She explained.

I smiled not because of what she said, but because my job wouldn't be so hard. I'd just kill the both of them and jet.

"Hold up handsome let me go get the telephone and don't you run." She told me.

Damn this bitch was making it easy, something about her just didn't feel right. She switched too hard and her hands were big for a woman.

'I might just be tired'. I thought.

I looked around for some photos, but it was dark in the small house. I was there to find a dude named Franky. Franky was about to get his cap peeled back. The lady came back with a cordless phone. I stepped in the living room and pretended to dial a number.

The lady was standing in the entrance batting those long eyelashes, licking her lips seductively.

"Goddizzamn!" I said to myself. This bitch had the longest tongue I'd ever seen. That shit was freaky, so freaky it turned me off.

A woman's tongue is not supposed to be that long. She kept rubbing her hand between her thighs. This bitch was trying to seduce me on the sneak tip. I peeped the move, I wasn't here for pleasure. After I pretended to mumble a few words, it was time for business. I handed her the phone back.

"Thank you, ma'am. My brother should come any minute." I said.

I had forgot that I was still wearing my gloves, until she said, "Nice glove, I like them." I looked at my hands, she licked her lips again with that snake tongue. "You can wait here. Would you like to have a seat? I can fix you some tea or coffee."

"No thank you, ma'am." I refused.

She licked those lips again, I decided to play along with her ass. I grabbed my dick and bit my bottom lip.

"Oooh… maybe I can handle that for you." She said in a way too deep voice. "By the way my name's Franky."

"What the fuck?" I said to myself almost aloud.

I was looking for a dude named Franky and this bitch's name was Franky. Then it hit me, the hairy stomach, the too large hands, the long masculine legs, and the fake eyelashes. This was a muthafuckin' twister. It was too dark to tell from the jump.

"Are you all right?" The punk asked.

I snapped out of it, "Yeah, I just thought I seen you somewhere before." I lied.

"Hmmm, where at handsome?" This nigga flirting now made me want to vomit.

"I think out Oxford Knoll one day."

"Oh, you might have, I got a little guy friend on the side named Moe."

At that moment, the faggot's telephone rang in my hands.

"I got this, it might be my brother calling back." I said. I disguised my voice. "Hello."

"Fraanky…oh Franky, Moe was killed tonight!" I hung up, it was another homosexual.

"Who was that?" Franky asked.

"He's outside," I replied.

Franky turned to look out the window. I pulled the Ruger P-89 from my pocket, pointed it to the punk's head, and pulled the trigger. Hunks of brain and skull flew on the side of the door and wall.

As he fell I shot him two more times in the side of the face and head. I pulled my ski mask down and calmly walked out the front door. Once I got to the street, Tree showed me, I bolted towards the curve. Rounding the curve, I saw the green Pontiac two cars up.

Tree was jogging towards his car. I got in, started the car, nodded at Tree, and drove off. Tree's Bonneville came flying pass me. That was the sign to follow him. I mashed the gas, after a maze of back streets, we ended up by Wheeler Road Southeast.

"What took you so long, Joe?" Tree asked.

"Man, you wouldn't believe that muthafucka Franky was a homo, Joe." I said.

"Nigga stop playing!" Tree said half believingly.

"The other joker I smashed tonight was fucking with that nigga on the side. He was a down low brother." I said.

"Damn, it's the days of our lives." Tree said. "Did you slump him?"

"Come on dog?" I looked at him smirking.

"Nothing, but dome shots, two to the head...two the head...two to the head...two to the head!" We both sang.

That was what the Go-Go band the Northeast Groovers banged.

"I'm about to bounce, just hit me on the hip," Tree said.

"A'ight Joe."

"Much love." He responded.

"Much love, nigga." I returned.

Tree peeled out, I drove back to my hood. I drove the car on Kelly Miller field and set it on fire. I was tired as shit, it had been one helluva night, but my mission was accomplished.

CHAPTER SEVEN

"Surprise!" I yelled.

"Nigga, where you been boy." Keisha screamed, as I walked in her front door.

Keisha ran and jumped on me, wrapping her legs around my waist, planting kisses all over my face. Keisha had on some tight black spandex tights, a little white T-shirt, and cute footie socks that was sexy as hell.

"Girl get your ass down." I playfully told her.

"Boy I haven't seen you in a week. I don't never want to let you go." Keisha said kissing me.

God, I felt like a King. Keisha pulled back and looked into my eyes. "Fox I really love you, boy." She said. "You just don't know how you brighten my days."

"Girl I missed you too." I said, tenderly kissing her soft lips.

Keisha hopped down off me, "Boo you hungry?"

"Nah, I'm straight." I said. "Come outside I gotta show you my new car."

"Ooooh... boy you got a new car?" She squealed. "Hold up let me put my shoes on."

Me and Keisha walked around back to the parking lot.

"Right there." I pointed at the midnight blue Caddy with the tints on the windows.

"Damn boy that muthafucka clean, come on let's go for a ride." She requested.

I walked up to the Caddy pretending to be a chauffeur and opened the passenger door. "Right this way ma'am." I joked in my best British imitation.

Keisha laughed. "Boy you so silly!"

Keisha sat down in the passenger seat, I walked around to the driver's side, got in, started the engine, and pulled off. We drove around for about an hour just talking.

I went to the carryout and brought us some food. Then we headed home, on the way to Keisha's house. We talked, and Keisha told me that she loved exotic fish. But, her mother would never get her any. She knew her mother was on drugs, but she wasn't ashamed. She was surprised at how I took it. I saw this type of shit every day, so it didn't bother me.

Keisha's house was damn near empty of furniture. I made a mental note to help them. As we were driving I heard sirens, I looked in the rearview mirror, it was the police.

"Damn." I said aloud.

"What's wrong?" Keisha asked worriedly.

"I got my gun on me, I ain't got a stash box in this joint yet. I just brought it. Fuck, I ain't going back down Oak Hill. I might have to run 'em." I told her.

"Shid... your ass ain't leaving me and I haven't seen you either." Kiesha said looking at me. "Hurry up give me the gun boy!" Keisha yelled.

I grabbed my gun and handed it to her. She slipped the gun in her waist band and pulled her shirt down.

"Damn this shorty gangsta." I told myself.

I pulled over, the police pulled up behind me, and walked up to my window. "License and Registration please."

I went into the glove compartment and got the necessary paper.

"Son how old are you?" He asked.

"I'm eighteen." I lied.

"Whose car is this?" He questioned.

"It's my step-father's car sir." I lied again.

"Where is your license?"

"I'ma be truthful sir, I don't have a license, I can give you my learners permit. I know I'm supposed to have somebody with a license with me. I just asked my step-father if I could drive to the carryout and get me and my honey dip some food." I knew throwing in the humor 'honey dip' would get this old ass officer.

He smiled, that was old folks slang. "Well son tonight's your lucky night if I search this car and find no drugs or illegal weapons. You and your honey dip can be on y'all way. If I find any drugs or weapons, you two will be going with me. Deal?" He insisted.

"Deal." I agreed.

My heart was racing because I didn't want Keisha to get caught with my gun. I made up my mind if he found that gun on Keisha I was going to try and kill him. Keisha had taken a big risk for me and I truly respected that.

I stepped out of the car and assumed the position. The officer patted me down thoroughly. He told Keisha to stay put, then he went inside the back-passenger door. He saw the food and felt it, thankfully it was still hot. So, that confirmed my story.

"My stomach is hurting really bad." Keisha groaned.

"You all right sweetheart?" I asked genuinely concerned.

Keisha had her face balled up in excruciating pain. The officer told her to get out and put her hands on the hood of the car.

"Are you all right, ma'am?" The officer asked.

"No, it's that time of the month." Keisha said.

"Oh, excuse me." Amazingly he didn't pat her waist, he just felt on the small of her back, when he saw her young plump voluptuous ass, he ran his hands down her tights.

That muthafucka could see she didn't have nothing down there, with his perverted old ass.

"Okay it's y'all lucky day, y'all free to go. Now drive safe." The officer said.

Once we got in the car and the officer pulled off I said, "Whoo wee, girl I was scared as shit."

"Shit I was gonna break on his ass if he would've felt this muthafucka." Keisha admitted.

"Love that was quick thinking. I thought you was for real." I informed her.

"You like that boo? You think I can be Cicely Tyson." Keisha asked.

"Damn right, you can be all them good actresses." I complimented.

Keisha kissed me on my cheek, I smiled.

"Here you go." Keisha handed me my gun and we drove back to her place.

CHAPTER EIGHT

When me and Keisha entered her apartment. Louise and Lawrence was in the kitchen smoking up a storm. They didn't even notice we had walked in the door.

"Come on." Keisha said.

We walked straight to her room, closed the door, and locked it. We ate our food, while sitting back watching T.V. Keisha's room was painted eggshell white, it had a little thirteen-inch color T.V. sitting on top of a big brown dresser. She had two twin beds, the room was small, but had a big window. The window looked damn near bigger than the room. I got up and sat in the window seal.

"What's wrong, boo?" Keisha asked.

"Nothing I'm just enjoying this view." I told her.

"What boy, you lunchin'. It ain't shit out there, but a parking lot wit' trash and vacant buildings." Keisha said.

"See Keisha I find beauty in the strangest places my eyes see some 'em different." I corrected her.

Keisha was quiet for a minute, then she said, "Damn you deep." I laughed. "Come over here and lay wit' me." She patted the bed.

I walked over and took my shoes off. I got in the bed and laid between her legs. Keisha immediately started playing in my hair.

"We gonna leave this shit one day." Keisha remarked.

"Yeah, I be thinking that too." I agreed.

"You had a rough life, I wanna make it easy Fox." Keisha said.

"I appreciate you for that." I told her.

Keisha leaned over and gave me a long sensuous kiss.

"Uummm…" she moaned.

"Girl don't start nothing you can't finished." I told her.

"Boy I can finish anything I start." She commented.

"Proceed then." I teased.

Keisha kissed me so passionately, I swear it felt like I was floating. My dick was bone hard. Keisha reached in my pants, wrapped her fingers around my dick, and started gently stroking me up and down.

"Ummm!" I groaned. "Damn girl."

"Take off your clothes." Keisha instructed.

I got up and quickly undressed. Keisha was already in her purple lace underwear. Damn she was so muthafucka sexy with those green eyes.

"Damn boy you got body!" Keisha moaned as I climbed back in bed.

"That came from all that working out with Greg and when I was locked up down Oak Hill."

I lifted Keisha's shirt and started lightly licking and sucking on her nipples. I heard her moan, my dick had pre-cum oozing out of the head.

Keisha stuck her index finger on the tip of my dick and started doing circular motions. That shit damn near made me nut in her hand. I sucked her titties harder.

"Put it in me." Keisha moaned.

I decided to prolong that request though, I stuck two fingers in her pussy. She was wet as an ocean, as I slid my fingers back and forth.

"Oohhh...Fox...oooh...boy!" Keisha whimpered, pulling me up to face her. "Stick it in." She whispered.

She looked so damn good, I wanted to eat her. I'd never ate pussy in my life, but I just wanted to please her after what she'd done for me tonight. I passionately tongue kissed her, Keisha tried to ease my dick in her, but I smoothly avoided entering her.

I kissed her forehead, then licked her chin all the way down to her neck.

"Take this shirt off." I instructed.

Keisha sat up and took the T-shirt off. Her big beautiful red titties with perfect brown nipples, sprang free. I licked her from her neck all the way down to the middle of her chest.

Keisha was shaking, "Oooh...bbb...baby!" She moaned.

I sucked on both of her pretty titties and continued to go down. I licked her from the top of her stomach to her navel. I blew in her navel and felt Keisha shaking. I continued to go down, I slid her underwear off, licked her hips, and dragged my tongue all way down to her inner thighs.

I could smell the aroma of her pussy. Keisha smelled like Heaven. I put my nose down there and sniffed.

My dick bounced so hard, it was hurting. I needed to be in her, but I held on. I lightly bit her between her thighs.

"Oooo...God!" Keisha moaned.

Keisha had both of her hands in my hair. I continued sucking her inner thighs, close to her pussy.

Keisha was so wet, her juices was running out of the slit of her pussy. I took two fingers and squeezed. Her juices flowed down her pussy towards her ass. Then I placed both of my thumbs on Keisha's pussy lips and spread them, as I stuck my tongue in her pussy as deep as it could go.

"Oooo...shit!" Keisha groaned.

I moved my tongue in and out and up and down, Keisha was humping my face.
"Aaahh...Fox...Boo...baby...dddamn!" She screamed.

I opened Keisha's pussy with my fingers and saw her clit. Just like in the Feen books I'd read when I was in Oak Hill. I gently blew on Keisha's clit. Keisha damn near pulled my hair out.

"Oh shit...oh shit...shit!" Keisha was panting heavily.

I wrapped my lips around her clit and gently licked and sucked, while finger fucking her.

Keisha had tears in her eyes,
"I'm...about...to...cum...Fox!" She cried.

"Cum in my mouth." I stopped and whispered. Then started licking back and forth real fast on her clit.

"I'm cumming…ooohhh…shit." Keisha got louder.

I stuck my tongue in Keisha's pussy and got to licking and sucking, as she came in my mouth. I tasted her scent, I was hyped. I worked my way back up and finally slid my dick in her.

"Goddamnnn!" Keisha was so tight and wet. Her pussy fit around my dick like a glove. Keisha hooked her arms underneath mine and dug her nails in my back.

"Open your eyes boo." Keisha whispered.

I opened my eyes to see her pretty green eyes staring at me seductively. She was biting her bottom lip.

"Oooh…I love you." Keisha said. "Tell me you love me." Keisha instructed, squeezing her pussy muscles even tighter. "I said tell me you love me." She ordered louder.

"I…I…love you girl!" I whispered. I felt like I was about to cum. "Hold up Keisha I don't have a rubber." I reminded her.

"Fox baby, I ain't fucking nobody else, plus I'm on the pill." Keisha informed.

"Nah I ain't tryna nut in you." I told her.

Keisha locked her legs around my waist, "Nigga this your pussy. I want you to nut in me, I want to feel you." She was persistent.

That shit turned me on, I grabbed Keisha's legs and put them over my shoulders. I started slamming my dick in her harder.

"Aaahhh…Fox…please…ooohhh. I'm cumming again!" She screamed.

My balls exploded and I started cumming deep inside of Keisha. I bent down and bit her neck, while I was cumming.

"Oh, shit boy, that shit felt good!" She squealed.

I rolled off her onto my back. I was breathing hard as fuck.

"Damn Fox you the first nigga that ever made me cum." Keisha admitted.

"Shid that was my first time eating pussy." I admitted.

"Stop playing, you lying." Keisha was astonished.

"Nah I swear, on my life." I told her.

"Damn you eat pussy like a professional." She complimented. We laughed.

"I had my pussy licked before, but not like that. I have a confession to make." Keisha eyed me. "I never sucked dick, but I'ma learn with you starting now." Keisha moved down and put my dick in her mouth.

Shiiid... I couldn't tell this was her first time. I think my dick grew solid in her mouth instantly. She licked the precum off my head and ran circles around my dick head, with her tongue.

I grabbed her head and laid back. Keisha swallowed me, she bobbed her head up and down.

"Umm...she groaned." Keisha started slurping and sucking faster.

"I'm 'bout to cum Keisha." I breathed.

Keisha kept sucking, until I started cumming in her mouth. "Ugghhh!" I groaned.

Keisha looked up at me, cum was running down the side of her chin.

"Damn this shit salty, but your ass mine, so I swallowed." She said.

My dick still hard, I told Keisha to get in the doggy style position. I entered her from the back. I started stroking her slow, Keisha moaned heavily. I told her to arch her ass in the air and put her face down. She did, just seeing her big pretty red ass, sent me over the edge. I held her small waist and pumped in and out of as fast as I could.

"Oh God…oooohhh." Kiesha was groaning with her face buried in the pillow.

I started hitting it faster and harder. "Arrgghh…damn girl." I groaned, as I started cumming again.

We both collapsed once we were finished and satisfied. We were so tired, we fell straight to sleep. We didn't even take a shower that night.

The next morning, we woke up and took a shower together. I bent Keisha over in the shower and hit it from the back. We both came, I put my clothes on and headed for the hood.

CHAPTER NINE

"Muthafucka where you been all night!" Big Doris yelled.

"Mama I fell asleep over my friend's house," I replied.

"Well your ass need to stay wit' your little friend." Big Doris fussed.

'Goddamn, do I ever get a break?' I thought.

It's always cussing and fussing whenever I come home late, early, evening, or whatever.

'Shit man.' I thought again. "Mama you need anything cause I'ma run to the store." I told her.

"Yeah, get me a pack of Kools and a bag of sugar." Big Doris replied.

She stopped arguing quick when I mentioned going to the store and asked if she needed anything. I went to my room, sat down on the bed, and put my head in my hands. I breathed easy, while sitting on the edge of my bed, my beeper went off. I looked at the number. I went into the living room and dialed the number back.

A woman's voice spoke, "Hello."

"Yeah somebody page me?" I asked.

"Yeah hold up," The woman replied.

"Hello, Squirrel." Nikki's voice came through the phone.

'Aaahh...shit'. I thought again.

"Baby where you been, I miss you." Nikki said.

"Nikki, girl you not entitled to call me baby no more. We just friend's." I reminded her.

"Squirrel, get serious me and you could never be friends." Nikki said. "Your ass belongs to me. So, what's up?" Nikki responded angrily.

"Maan...I ain't got time for this, Nikki. I just been chilling. I'ma holla at you, I gotta go to the store for my mama." I said.

"You think it's a joke Squirrel. I know where you were at last night. If I catch you with that little green-eyed bitch I'ma stab you and her muthafuckin' ass." *Click!* Nikki hung up.

"What the fuck is up wit' these bitches thinking they own me?" I asked myself. I shook the thought off, got up, and walked out of the door.

"What's up slim?" Tye greeted me.

I gave Tye some dap. "Ain't shit soldier, what's up around this joint?" I asked.

"Man it's been slow, but you know the early bird gets the warm." Tye replied.

"Yeah, slim."

"Ho…hold up Tye…hey Fast Mike." I yelled. "Hey fast Mike!"

Fast Mike was a dark-skinned skinny crackhead who walked so fast, we called him Fast Mike.

He would run errands for us, like going to the store. Fast Mike was the neighborhood delivery boy. He walked so fast that when we would send him to the carryout to order us food, he'd come back with our food, still hot. Fast Mike had an amazing memory too, we would do shit on purpose, like order a ridiculous amount of food. Fast Mike didn't even have to write anything down. He would remember everything we told him to order.

I mean everything, even the two pepper packs, we threw in just to confuse him. He never missed an order. Fast Mike was serious about his job and getting that crack rock.

"Hey Mike…suit and boots, I got some 'em' for you Joe." I said.

Mike came rushing over there, "What's up shorty?" Mike said in his beady voice. I decided to hype him up, when I saw he had on some new sneakers.

"Goddizzamn… Fast Mike, what's dem joints?" I asked feigning in awe.

"Oh, these are some pro wings youngin'." Mike was grinning from ear to ear. "I had to step it up."

I almost died laughing, but I had to maintain my composure. At first, Fast Mike had some run-down dress shoes. Them joints were leaning to the fifth degree. Now he had some semi-new tennis shoes.

"Oh Youngsta, I miss my Benny heels though." Mike said.

Benny heels was the name we'd affectionately given his old dress shoes(penny loafers).

"Mike, I promise one day I'ma take you down Georgetown and let you pick out any dress shoes you want." I told him.

"For real, youngsta." Mike asked excitedly.

"Yeah Fast Mike, you got my word on it." I replied.

"Awe man, Youngsta see that's why I fucks wit' you. You never done Fast Mike wrong. You ain't like all these other Youngstas."

Now Fast Mike was pouring it on thick.

"Hey Mike, I need you to run to the store for me." I said.

"Ah okay whatcha need? You know Fast Mike gotcha." This bama was Bo jangling hard.

"Peep, I need a pack of Kools and a bag of sugar for Big Doris. Make it quick cause I gotta bounce." I requested.

"Okey Dokey." Fast Mike agreed.

I handed him a twenty-dollar bill. "Keep the change hustler." I instructed.

"Ah man thank you, Youngsta. Fast Mike will be straight back." He replied smiling even harder.

He zipped off before I had a chance to say anything else. Knowing him he'd probably steal the bag of sugar and buy the cigarettes. So, what as long as he brought back my shit.

As me and Tye sat down on the maze wall. Pipe heads started coming from everywhere, it started pumping on the strip.

"Fuck dis, I need some yay." I said.

"Don't rush yourself." Tye suggested.

"Nigga I guess you would say that, you out this bitch making a killing." I reminded Tye.

"Well don't blame me Reagan started this shit, I'm just finishing it...my yay that is." Tye remarked.

I busted out laughing, this nigga Tye was crazy. Fast Mike was back within minutes.

"Damn Joe you back already? What you got a hidden bike or something." I asked.

"Nah, baby boy Fast Mike do his job and do it well. I don't question you about your B.I. so I humbly ask that you respect mine." Fast Mike stated.

I couldn't believe this bama, I had to laugh it off. That was his duty and he had a right to take his job seriously.

****

I took Big Doris her items and came back outside. The maze was crowded with niggas now hustling,shooting dice and talking shit. Only niggas who lived down there was allowed.

Other sections of the hood respected each other. If you were a good nigga, you were clear to hustle anywhere. Omar, Ronald, Boo-Boo, Domo, Ralph, Greg, Black Mike, Twon, Lil Feet Kevin, Toot, Big Franky, Frank, Dirk, and a gang of other hustlers was down in the maze.

They had started a big dice game. I was sitting on the high low wall in the maze just observing. This was all my hood, all love, niggas talking shit, betting money, and looking fly, I lived for this shit right here.

"Nigga I'ma shoot the number off these bitches." Boo-Boo was shouting.

It was his dice and he was betting Domo. Domo was standing there with a stack of money in his hand, and a pile of money on the ground. Boo-Boo was on his hands and knees in all brand-new clothes. I had gone and got my hamma 'cause you never know when drama would jump off.

"Who...Whooo. Track stars...track stars!"

Oh, shit that was the code for the jump outs. I quickly looked around and saw them running up the back side. Niggas broke in all directions.

Boo-Boo and Domo were the last to run because they had been collecting their money. Boo-Boo broke one way and Domo the other. I was watching the jump-outs chase them. I was about to get off the wall when Domo came running back around the corner full speed.

Domo was haulin' ass, two jump outs had him trapped. One had appeared in front of Domo and one was still chasing him. With the agility of a football player, Domo ran toward the officer who appeared in front of him.

Both officers surely thought he was caught. Domo juked left, then right, and spun out of the officer's reach. The officer that had been chasing him was so busy trying to follow his moves, he clipped up on his own feet and fell face first.

The whole hood yelled, "Ooohhh..."

Domo was swift as a cheetah, I started walking towards my building.

"Hey, you stop right there. Put your hands in the air!" The jump-out yelled. It was a fuckin' woman.

"Shit!" I groaned under my breath. I stopped and threw my hands in the air.

She had her police issued Glock trained on me. One false move and I was dead. D.C. police were known to shoot your ass.

"Get down there." She ordered.

I looked, and niggas was line up with their arms and legs spread on the wall. A jump-out was searching all of them confiscating shit.

"Oh, shit I got this hamma on me." I mumbled.

I went down there, spread my arms, and legs on the wall too. As the jump-out woman walked past she said, "Well…well Lil' Fox we finally meet in person."

I looked back and she was too pretty to be a damn police. She had on a red bandanna, army pants, and track hi tec boots. She was light brown-skinned, with dark long eyelashes, and a curvy shape.

Damn she was cute as hell, but there was no time for this, I had to focus.

"My name Lisa, Lil' Fox." She informed. "I've heard a lot about you. You just coming home from Oak Hill, huh? Well today your elusive ass might be going back. Stay here and don't move. We also heard your brother Big Fox is out Maryland on a murder charge. Too bad we couldn't stick one to him here."

"Dirty bitch." I whispered.

"Huh, speak up. I didn't hear you." She turned back around.

"I ain't say nothin'." I mumbled.

"Oh, okay, I didn't think so." She spat.

I'ma punish this bitch, she bet not ever let me catch her slipping. I'ma show her ass since she like playing dirty locking muthafuckas up.

"Man, what the fuck you doing?" Twon yelled.

"Where you get all this money from?" One jump-out officer asked.

"Man, I saved my shit." Twon responded.

"Nah wrong answer." Said the jump-out as he threw Twon's money in the air.

"Man!" Twon screamed.

The wad of hundred-dollar bills went flying in the air in all directions. That was my cue, now it was my turn to get ghost.

I bolted, I was through the cut. When Lisa shouted. "Halt...halt!"

I was down shifting, I was in fourth gear turning the corner. They wasn't catching me.

I heard somebody say, "Damn Squirrel gone, that nigga fast like a squirrel too."

"Catch him...catch him!" Lisa shouted.

I headed down the back street, toward the woods. I knew if I hit the woods I was ghost, but if they followed pursuit it could be my life. They could shoot and kill me, it would be justified homicide because I got this pistol on me.

I entered the woods like a runaway slave running for freedom. I took a peak back they were coming, but they were too far back. I'd ran these woods for years, they'd never catch me. I headed for Dead Man's tunnel.

"Call the K9 unit." I heard one of the officer's yell.

"Too late homie." I said. "I'm outta here." I hopped the booby trap ditch, ducked a low branch, and slid down the hill by the creek where the tunnel was.

"Officer down...officer down!" A police officer shouted.

I fought back laughter because I knew one of them dumb ass jump-outs had fallen in the hole that's been there for years. If you didn't work the woods you were prone to get fucked up. Bobbie traps was all over that joint.

Even the dope fiends and crackheads knew about the traps. The traps secured them, it was a hood secret that we took to heart. I heard a walkie talkie cackle.

"We have one in pursuit, dark blue sweat jacket, black jeans, brown boots, and a black wave cap. We...officer down...another officer down!"

Another police officer was down, I started laughing as I kept running. *Pop...pop...*awe shit they were shooting at me now. Two officers down they were mad. Fuck 'em I didn't have time to play supa nigga. That would be idiotic.

I reached the big tunnel in the creek. I used to run through as a kid. I heaved with a heavy push and hurried up and slid through the massive steal gate. The gate had to weigh at least five hundred pounds. When we were young and used to run the woods, it would take four of us to push and swing the massive gate.

I was strong enough now to do it by myself. It was pitch black in the tunnel. Creek water flowed through it to the other side. You had to stay close to the wall, if you didn't you'd slip in the slippery moss water.

If you fell you were subjected to fall on anything, needles, dead bodies, feces...*anything*. I stuck my fingers on the wall and ran, I was used to this routine, so I could run full speed. I was safe cause I knew the jump-outs didn't see where I had run at. I came out on the other side. I was scott free, my pants from the knees down was soaking wet. I decided not to go directly back to the hood. I'd wait for about an hour, until everything cooled off.

As I was walking in the back path of Aton Elementary School. I could see the street, I saw a black cocky dude sitting on a black 280 Z. He was talking to another dude, it was the bitch ass nigga Hairio. The nigga that was laughing and talking shit at the dice game that day Mohammad shot at me.

Damn, I could've busted his brains right now and get away with it. Hairio didn't even see me or wasn't paying attention. Niggas bumped heads on an unexpected basis. That was why you couldn't get caught slipping, and he was definitely slipping. I started to creep towards the street, then I stopped, as I watched him sit on his car and play big. I was on another mission, so today was his lucky day. I slid back into the darkness and left.

CHAPTER TEN

"Hey love." I said as I answered my cell phone. I knew it was my baby.

"Boy how did you know it was me?" Keisha asked.

"You the only girl that's calling me." I responded.

"I better be." She retorted.

"You are boo, what's up wit'cha?" I replied.

"Ain't shit." Keisha said.

"Look Boo," I started. "I need you to do something for me." I continued.

"Whatever you need boo." Keisha said.

"I need you to pick up something over my aunt Tinan's house. I can't do it cause I'm tied up right now. I'm glad you called too, you right on time." I told her. "My aunt said she has some important papers for me, but I've been too busy to go over there."

"Okay, I'ma stop through on my way to Peaches house today." Kiesha agreed. "I'm about to leave now. That's why I was calling, so you could come pick me up later on tonight." She said.

"Got that."

"I'm at the bus stop now." Keisha told me. "Oh, baby my bus coming, I'll call you later. I love you." Keisha hurriedly said.

"Love you too." I rushed to tell her before she hung up.

Keisha didn't know I'd peeped her routine. Every Thursday, she went over Peaches house to get her hair done. I knew she'd be gone all day and I had a surprise for her. I hurriedly got in my caddy and drove over Keisha's house.

When I got there the house was empty, just like I told Louise to have it. I pulled out my cell phone and called my personal crackhead Kevin. I had brought all his old furniture from him. Kevin sold me everything for four hundred dollars' worth of crack. The furniture was practically brand new. I brought a long brown couch, a matching love seat, and a single chair.

I brought four big funny shaped lamps, a glass coffee table, a decent stereo system, with four speakers and an amp, a CD and tape deck. I also brought two small brown tables with a matching big table.

Kevin said he was refurnishing his apartment, but I knew he owed a bill that he wasn't going to pay, because I had given crack for this shit. I had also ordered a bedroom set from the neighborhood boasters. It was Keisha's favorite color purple and black.

I had gotten Kevin to bring everything around to Keisha's apartment on the back of his truck. Once Kevin arrived, me, him, and Lawrence, Keisha's crackhead step-father unloaded the furniture and took into Keisha's apartment.

After every piece of furniture was in place, Keisha's place looked brand-new. It looked real cozy, nice, and neat. I stepped back and admired my handy work. I loved Keisha, so I wanted to make her happy. I told Kevin to go pick up Robin, another crackhead around Lincoln Heights, who cleaned houses for crack, and she was nice with interior decorating.

Robin arrived, I told her to clean and put the bedroom set up that I'd brought.

"Ooohhh… baby you gonna like how I hooked ya sweetheart's room up." Robin replied.

Robin had finished her job, I went in Keisha's room and looked in awe. Robin had changed the sheets, to the colors black and purple. She put the black curtains in the windows, all the clothes were neatly hung in the closet and all the dirty clothes were in the matching purple hampers.

She had put cheap paintings on the walls with little glow lights to give it a relaxing effect. The two brown tables were on each side of the twin beds with the purple and black lamps. It was really nice, I nodded my head in satisfaction. For my last effect, I had Kevin and Lawrence carry the big oval shaped fish tank in Keisha's room. They sat it on the table right between the twin beds. I had bought eight exotic colorful fish.

The background of the fish tank was so beautiful, it had all types of color images of Atlantis. The little fish loved their new home. They just swam back and forth happily. Everything I'd bought to make over Keisha's apartment had cost me five hundred dollars, but the smile on her face was going to be priceless.

"Baby you like it?" Robin asked.

"Oh yeah," I said mesmerized. "It's so beautiful, what you want money or crack?"

"Baby you can give me whatever. I'm not picky." Robin replied.

Damn she sure knew how to soft stroke a nigga when doing business. She'd done a tremendous job, so I blessed her.

"Here you go Robin." I handed her a fifty rock and a fifty-dollar bill.

Robin's eyes got big as hell, "Ooh thank you son-son." She said excitedly as she hugged me.

I called Lawrence into the room and handed him two twenty rocks.

"Thanks man." Lawrence said.

I personally didn't like Lawrence, he gave me a bad feeling.

"Alright everybody time to go." I hollered. "Okay, assume the position." I ordered when they got to the door.

Kevin already knew the routine, he put his hands in the air as I patted him down. "Drop ya pants."

Kevin dropped his pants and jumped up and down.

"Alright take your shoes and socks off." Kevin complied, and I let him out the door. He knew we searched pipe heads in our crack houses for anything stolen.

Robin looked at me like I was crazy. I told her to strip ass naked and if she had anything that belonged to Keisha or anybody in this apartment, I was taking my money and crack back.

"Baby you ain't got to do that." Robin said.

"Yeah but you from the hood, you know the routine. Ain't shit changed and don't get brand new." I told her.

She stripped ass naked and jumped up and down. I peeped Lawrence looking at her titties and ass as they jingled. I smirked, Robin was clean, I patted Lawrence down just to show that I had no picks.

After everybody was out of the house I told Lawrence to go find Louise and bring her back. I bid Kevin and Robin farewell as they drove back around the hood.

"Oh, good God." Keisha's mother Louise said when she opened the door and saw her apartment.

"Fox baby I can't thank you enough. I'ma really try to straighten myself up. I know I've been smoking and fucking up. I never met nobody who was as generous as you. You really love my daughter huh? Woo, I'm glad she met you." Louise went on and on.

"Lawrence do you see all this, and do you see what he did to Keisha's room? The big fish tank wit' fish and all." Louise asked Lawrence.

"Yeah I helped too." Lawrence said in his goofy ass voice that irritated me.

Lawrence was biting his nails, that nigga was trying to smoke that rock I'd gave him.

"Go ahead and do your thang." I told Lawrence.

Louise cut her eye at Lawrence. "Oh, muthafucka you weren't gonna tell me you had some 'em huh?" Louise smacked Lawrence on top of the head. "Now come on."

Lawrence looked at me like, '*Damn, why you say something*'?

I put my hands up in a silent apology. "My bad."

Pipe heads were some cruddy muthafuckas. Right then as my thoughts roamed Keisha called.

"Hey, baby your aunt wasn't home when I dropped by." She said.

I had already known that, but I was stalling her for time. "Are you ready for me to come get you?" I asked.

"Yeah, I'm up Peaches house."

"A'ight I'm on my way." I hung up.

I was excited like a child on Christmas morning. I drove over Stevenson Road Barryfarms southeast and picked Keisha up. She looked good, she had her hair done in micro braids. She had on a cream flower shirt, tight black jeans, and leather rider boots.

Damn my girl was killin' em. As I drove up I saw all the hated stares from the neighborhood youngins, but I was a real goon, packing heat too, so that made me just as dangerous as them. I got out of the car and kissed her, just so the niggas knew this was my bun-bun.

As me and Keisha got in the car, I threw my *Scarface* CD in, '*The World Is Yours*', turned the volume up and let the bass to '*Always Look A Man In The Eye Before You Kill 'Em*, blasted in my caddy. As the speakers hummed the tune, I drove in slow motion, so they could hear, that good drama music.

As I stopped at the stop sign, I thought it was gonna be on. The dudes were deep as hell at the corner, I had tints on my windows, so I told Keisha to duck down as I pulled the Mac 10 from under my seat. I clicked the safety off, put it in my hand, and leaned my seat back as far as it would go.

Keisha asked no questions, she ducked down as far as she could go. If a nigga even threw a rock at my car, I was gonna spray these muthafuckas like roaches. I know niggas be doing all type of crazy shit when you fucking a broad they like. I ain't going for that, I rolled my window down and rolled my back windows halfway down, so they could look inside the car. It was a sign of respect, them niggas were gangstas.

They recognized what I did and nodded. Everybody was respectful except one short, chubby, dark-skinned nigga. He looked like he wanted to pull out on me.

"Go head Young, try ya hand and ya feathers gonna get plucked." I mumbled.

After I acknowledged all the dudes, I turned and drove outta there. I was glad there was no confrontation.

"You can sit up now." I told Keisha.

"Boy what was that all about?" She asked.

"It was a territory thing." I replied. "Hey, look back, you see that little chubby dark-skinned dude?" I asked.

"Yeah." Keisha nodded.

"Who dat?"

"Oh, that's Rob he likes me." She confirmed.

It never failed, I had to make note of that. Shorty was going to be a problem, but not for me because if he jumped his family was gonna be paying for his funeral.

"I have a surprise for you." I told Keisha when I pulled up in front of her apartment building.

"What boo...what?" Keisha questioned excitedly.

"Come with me my dear." I said in a British accent.

Keisha busted out laughing. "Boy you are so stupid."

I hooked my right arm in her left arm, tucked the Mac 10, and began to march. Keisha couldn't stop laughing, I always loved to play and joke with Keisha. She had the most beautiful smile. When we approached her building, I saw some dudes watching me and Keisha joke around.

Keisha was beautiful, every nigga wanted to slide his dick in her fine ass. I kept doing what I was doing, because one thing I knew for sure was that looks didn't hurt, but bullets do. I covered Keisha's eyes as we walked through her door.

Then I let go. "Ta-daaa." I said.

Keisha looked around, she was speechless, then she said. "Oh my God, Fox boy you brought all this furniture?"

"Yup, I did it for the house." I responded smiling.

"This is the best surprise I ever had. Nobody ever thought about me like this." Keisha said.

"Nah, your surprise is in your room." I corrected.

Keisha looked at me, then walked to her room, once she hit the light switch the glow of the painting and the laps illuminated the room, while the big fish tank glowed.

Keisha started screaming with joy, "Ooooh…my gawd, Fox…oh, my gawd!" Keisha was panting.

I walked behind her, "Baby calm down before you catch an asthma attack."

She saw the fish tank and ran over to it, "Oooo…Fox boo the fish are so cute. Look at that little one, and that cute one over there…oooh, I'ma name that one Fox and that one Squirrel."

I stood there watching Keisha, she was so excited, she was already naming the fish. I hadn't felt this proud in my life, I felt I had really accomplished something.

Keisha suddenly stopped naming fish and just stared at the tank. I closed the room door and walked up beside her. Keisha was crying hysterically. I picked her up and hugged her tight. I stroked her back up and down.

"Baby I know…I know." I whispered in her ear.

"Fox nobody, ever done this for me." She cried. "You remembered that I liked fish, but my mother would never buy me any." Keisha grabbed me tighter.

"Boy, I love you so much! Do you hear me?" She asked through clenched teeth.

Damn I felt like crying myself, "I love you too, that's why I did all this for you, love." I whispered. "You opened a part of me, I thought was closed forever." I told her.

I felt her hug me tighter. "Fox, I know what you be doing in them streets. I need you here with me, please be careful."

"Baby life ain't promised, so I can't promise anything, but I'll try." I swore to her.

Me and Keisha laid down and made passionate love, expressing our emotions. Keisha put her hands on my chest as she was riding me, I tried to hold her waist, she stopped me.

"No baby just lay back and let me please you." She demanded.

I held the headboard as Keisha rode me, her pussy was wet and tight. I felt I was about to explode, Keisha felt it too. She planted her palms on my chest and bounced her ass.

"Ahhh.I was lost in estacy. Keisha's face and happiness today, was priceless.

CHAPTER ELEVEN

A jury found Snuk not guilty and he came home. I had brought him a red Mountain bike for his welcome home gift. I knew he liked bicycles, plus he wasn't hurting for money. I went over the details about Moe and the homosexual Franky. Snuk laughed until he couldn't breathe.

"Nigga you crazy." Snuk said. "Man, I gots to make some rounds and I gotta go see my kids. I'll holla at you lil' bro. You be safe out here, you hear me?" Snuk said.

"Yeah bro." I answered.

"Ooh, I heard what Mohammad did. If I don't kill him first, you know you got the green light on his ass."

"That's mandatory." I said lifting my shirt to show him the compact Glock .40 with extended clip.

"Damn Squirrel, you not playing lil bruh'." Snuk sounded shocked.

"You can't be in these times. I saw Hairio last week, I could have killed him, but the jump-outs was chasing me through the tunnel. When I came out on the back path, I peeped him sitting on his car talking to some bama. I could have down him, but I was on another mission."

"You did right, Joe. I'm proud of your thinking." Snuk said. "But you know your name is getting out there so niggas gonna want to kill your name before they kill you." Snuk informed. "So, don't fuck up out here, jealousy and envy are best friends. Then hate will kill you because it's killing them. Handle your affairs and lay low for a minute. Make sure you save your money because you gonna need it. We at war, all day, every day whether you feel it or not." Snuk said.

"Keep your vest on physically as well as mentally. I'm out, I'll holla in a week or so." Snuk said, just before he peeled off, he stopped and looked at me.

"Just remember I'ma ghost, if you can't see me, you can't touch me." With that said he disappeared around the corner.

I sat there and thought about what he said, Snuk was deep. I admired the game he spat, I wore his jewels proudly.

****

Friday morning, I was up bright and early, things was going smooth around the hood. I haven't been around here in a while. I had been playing Keisha's spot tough. Spending all my money up playing big and shit. I only came home to sleep, shower, and was gone again.

Snuk said as long as a nigga didn't see you, he couldn't touch you. I tried to physically live his philosophy. It was deeper than the physical though, I came to understand that later.

I took a shower, put on some black jeans, my red and dark blue pull over, and my black and white Air Force Ones. I grabbed my pistols and was out.

I walked outside, today was a nice day, but it was too quiet. I backed up in my hallway and pulled out a pistol. I peeked both ways and waited, I didn't see nobody. That's what alerted my spider senses.

There was usually a pipe head or cat running through this place. I waited fifteen minutes, then I stepped out, when I stepped I saw pipehead Pet in her hallway in the next building. I felt better, then I saw Carlise's fine ass sitting on her front porch. My Caddy was parked right in front of her building

"What's up Carlise?" I spoke, walking to my car.

"Heeyy...Squirrel wit' ya bad self." She replied smiling.

I blushed like a girl. "Damn I gotta stop this lil' boy blushing shit." I told myself.

I opened my car door and got in, I started it, and let it warm up. I wanted to hear my *Scarface* tape, I looked all around until I found it, under my arm rest.

As I put it in and was searching for my song, my intuition told me to get underneath my steering wheel. This time I listened to my first thought.

Tires screeched to a halt! Pop…Pop…Pop…gun shots rang out.

My car window exploded, shattered glass flew everywhere, *Plop…Plop…*the shots continued. I was crouched all the way under my dashboard. The car was trembling from the shots, I felt blood running down my face.

"Aah shit I'm hit." I mumbled, blood was everywhere.

SQUEERK… I heard tires peel off and the car speeding off. I stayed put for about a minute. I had my gun in hand, as I finally got out of the car. I was in such shock that my body started shaking and I collapsed.

"Aaahhh…oh my God!" I heard Carlise scream. "They shot Squirrel! They shot Squirrel!" She cried out .

Pipehead Pet came running over to me, "Baby…baby! Are you alright?" I tried to get up. "No baby, you need an ambulance." Pet said soothingly.

I got up anyway, I checked myself all over. I realized, I wasn't shot, the glass from the shattered windows had flew in my forehead and face, cutting me up. All that blood looked like I had been shot. I took my Gortex jacket off, some people were saying sit him down, he hurt. But I wasn't hurt, I was now mad.

"A nigga tried to kill me!" I realized I still had time to catch 'em. "What kinda car was they in Carlise?" I hollered.

She was still crying, "A gray Buick, it was two of them and a white Malibu following behind them."

"I'm alright!" I yelled out.

Someone had brought me some wet towels. I wiped my forehead. I looked at my Caddy and that vehicle looked like swiss cheese. There were holes everywhere in my driver and passenger door.

Whoever shot at me punished my ride severely. These niggas were amateurs wit' this shit. All them shots and I didn't get hit one time. That was a blessing, these cowards must have been shooting with their heads turned. If they would have paid attention they would have saw I wasn't in the seat. My tints also helped save me, cause they couldn't fully see inside the car. I was so mad that tears started falling from my eyes. Niggas started coming out now with pistols in their hands.

"Squirrel, you all right?"

"Squirrel who did it?"

"Squirrel what happened?"

With all the questions niggas were asking me. I was so mad, I couldn't even answer. I grabbed my hamma, jumped in the car and peeled out. I was determined to catch the niggas who tried to take my life. They couldn't have drove too far, I took all the back streets. I knew that was the way they'd take.

The Caddy big V8 roared, I was flying at ninety miles per hour down little streets. After about thirty minutesor longer of looking, I past an alley on an isolated back street. I saw what looked like a grey Buick. I stepped on the brakes and busted a U-turn, as I drove back past, there it was with two dudes in it.

I couldn't believe it. All I knew in my head was I couldn't give these dudes a second chance at the dice. I grabbed my glock and drove a little further down. I knew this street like the back of my hand. I'd come down here at times and sat in my car thinking.

I got out and ran on the side of a vacant houses. I could cut through there and come out on the side of them. This was too good to be true, because the car the two dudes was sitting in was right next to the vacant house.

I was up on them now, I could see that both of them, smoking a blunt. They had on all black clothing. I couldn't hear what they were saying, but I could see them laughing. The guy on the passenger side lifted his hands. That's when I saw the gun, he was imitating how he was shooting. Damn these niggas were talking about me. I stepped out from between the vacant house, they were still talking. I wanted them to see me, when I was three steps away from the passenger side door, they saw me.

The blood on my forehead,the anger in my face,the blood had dried up and was now crusty, my shirt was heavily specked with blood. I knew I looked crazy, I had my gun trained on them. They looked like they had seen a ghost.

BOOM!...BOOM!..BOOM!..BOOM!..BOOM! The canon rang out loud as I fired shots into both of them.

The fire from the barrel of the gun was blinding. The first throng of bullets cut the passenger's face in half. The driver tried to scream but no words came out.

The gun echoed in the small alley, the driver's head was stuck to the side door. Brain matter was all over the car, and the sick copper smell of raw blood was thick. I was about to leave then I turned back around and walked up to the car. I looked inside and saw the passenger side was painted red.

I used my shirt to open the door, the body fell out. I looked inside and saw the gun, it was a Beretta .9mm. I picked it up, I went to the driver's side, opened the door, the body was stinking, this nigga had shitted on himself.

I searched his body, he had some weed, three hundred and fifty dollars, and some condoms, but no gun. He had on all black leather. I hurriedly took the jacket off him. This was going to be a message for whoever sent them. The leather jacket was bloody, but I still took it. I'ma wash this then take it to the cleaners. I grabbed the money and left the weed. I used my shirt for handling all the items. I took the items and ran back between the house to my car.

I hated to get rid of my car, but I knew I would have too. I drove to the edge of the alley, I stopped, got out, popped my trunk, and grabbed the gasoline can I kept. I ran up to the Buick and hurriedly dashed it with gas.

I dosed the bodies too, then I lit the lighter that was in the grey Buick, I lit the bodies and car aflame. I hurriedly ran back to my car and balled out. I was satisfied then, justice was done, but I didn't feel good about it.

I had taken all my shit out of my Caddy and burnt it up. That was a good car and I loved it, but I knew I couldn't keep it. Even if I got it sealed up and repainted. One of the bullets had been lodged in the engine and it was slipping anyway.

I said goodbye to my Caddy, I was back on foot now. Times had gotten hard for me, I knew that things had taken a drastic turn. My money was low, I had no car, and Big Doris was on my back like a tight tank top. I'd been shot at and almost killed in the last couple of weeks. Me and Snuk were now beefing with a Simple City dude. His beef was also my beef, I was so depressed. Keisha had gone to care for her sick grandmother out in Maryland.

My buddies were somewhere attending to their own business and I was definitely lost.

CHAPTER TWELVE

"What's happening Squirrel?" Ralph asked.

"Ain't shit Joe, just maintaining." I answered.

Ralph was my neighbor from the building next door. His mother Bren was my god-mother, she always looked out for me and Snuk.

"Man, I heard you had some drama wit' them bamas down the back street, Mohammad and them." Ralph said. "He paid some jokers to smash you."

"What." I said under my breath. *'So that's who them niggas was who shot up my Caddy. That was Mohammad's work, huh? Bitch ass nigga, I should've known I didn't think Mohammad's coward ass would go so far. Now that nigga had got big headed.'*

"Squirrel!" Ralph hollered, snapping me out of my thoughts.

"Yeah, Joe." I responded.

"You know Big Fox been laying low and you the only nigga still in the hood. Are you crazy or just fucking stupid?" Ralph stated.

"Nigga I ain't got no place to hide, plus I ain't duckin' no drama." I answered.

"Squirrel, you can go lay at a rack of spots. Stop denying yourself young, your buddies ain't out in the jungle like you. Look at you, you done turned into an animal. The only buddy you got that's putting it down is yo man Black Mike and he's as elusive as a black cat. You rarely see him, but you hear of his work. I admit Squirrel yougin' you go hard, but don't die going hard. You a young soldier wit' a good heart. Don't get stopped out here, the streets love nobody. I love you like a little brother. Just be careful, *young*." Ralph stepped off.

I stood there and thought for a minute, the things Ralph had said didn't do anything but fuel my fire. This bitch ass nigga Mohammad had the audacity. I called myself rocking this bama to sleep, but he wasn't going for the okie doke rock move. Well, I had to come out the wood work, but I was dead broke with no coke to sell. Things had slowed down.

"Fuck." I grumbled.

Two eleven was definitely about to be in progress, I really didn't want to be a robber because it was a lot of work, but I was broke. Money was a must, to be able to war.

Li-Poo had come to like my hood, he got to hang out wit' some wild young niggas like my man Adrian. Adrian and Li-Poo smoked weed together all day. He didn't get to meet the real rough necks though. He was in many presences, but never knew this circle could be so vicious.

We were out in front of my man Sco's building, the same building Ralph lived in. Me, Li-Poo, my man Sco, Juicy, Boo-Boo, Omar, Ty, Greg, and Ronald.

We all were out there joking around. On the third floor a new broad had moved into Apartment 32 on the right-hand side. Her name was Tammy, she'd been living here for about eight months. She was short, brown-skinned, with an Anita Baker hair style, and her ass was phat as a cow.

Tammy had ass for days, she also had two kids. She and I became real cool, Tammy was cool, she used to invite me to her apartment to chill with her.

I told her that I had a girl and I loved my girl, she was cool with that. One day I went to Tammy's apartment just to chill out.

No one was home except Tammy's little sister who was also sexy as hell and looked fine as a muthafucka. I ended up falling asleep on the couch, I opened my eyes to find Tammy pulling me off the couch. I was dead beat tired, the stress of the streets had worn me down. I hadn't realized, I hadn't been getting any sleep, until that day.

Tammy pulled me up and walked me into her bedroom. She laid me down and took my shoes off. I felt her unbutton my pants and take my shirt off. I was too tired to protest, I just wanted to lay down in the bed.

I remember laying down and Tammy lying next to me. I was sleeping good as a baby. About three hours into my sleep, I felt something rubbing against me. I jumped but found myself pinned down. I was about to panic, the first thing I thought was this bitch set me up.

"Boy just lay back." I heard Tammy whisper.

My vision came into focus and I realized, it was Tammy on top of me, kissing my chest nipples.

"Mmmm…" Tammy moaned.

"Tammy, I told you I got a girl." I reminded.

"Not now nigga." She replied and kept kissing my body.

"Look I can't do this." I repeated.

"Do what…you already doing it!" Tammy squeezed her pussy muscles and I felt the warm sensation of wetness around my dick.

"I finally got your ass where I want you Fox. I been waiting to get you for so long. Now, I got you." Tammy started bouncing her ass up and down on my dick. "Tell me this pussy ain't good…tell me." She commanded.

I couldn't say a word because the pussy was good. I found myself humping her back.

"Yeah baby that's right, don't be afraid to fuck me. Yeah this your pussy now." She moaned. I held Tammy's hip and started pumping. "Ooooh…shit, Fox damn boy."

"You want me to fuck you huh?" I asked.

"Yeah." she moaned louder.

"Turn this ass around." I ordered.

Without getting off my dick, Tammy turned around. Now her ass was facing me and riding me backwards cowgirl style. I spread her ass cheeks and pump hard and fast.

"Woo…wooo…woooo…" Tammy moaned.
"Aahh…baby, why you doing me like this. Ooohhh…I'm

cumming...unnhhh." Tammy moaned more intensely as I kept fucking her.

I felt her juices running down the side of my balls. I was about to nut.

"Tammy get up girl, I'm 'bout to nut." I said.

"Nut in me...nut in me." She begged.

"Argghh...shit!" I groaned as I started cumming.

Tammy grinded away as I came in her. Tammy laid her back on my chest while my dick was still in her. I rubbed my hands over her beautiful body. I felt her titties and played with her nipples.

"Oohh...baby." Tammy whispered.

She got up and went down, she looked up at me with those sexy bedroom eyes, then slid my dick in her mouth.

"Damn!" I mumbled..

My dick grew to its length, Tammy kept sucking. I grabbed her hair and humped her mouth. I thought she was going to gag, but she took it all. I felt myself on the verge of cumming, Tammy's throat game was good.

"Aaahh...Tammy I'm...bout...to..." I couldn't even finish my sentence.

"Cum then!" She mumbled, with her mouth full of dick.

I let go as she sucked harder, that shit felt so good, I went straight to sleep.

"Your ass mine now." Is the last thing I heard Tammy say before passing out.

I woke up to the smell of fried eggs and pancakes. I got up and my plate was sitting on the night stand next to the bed.

"That's you boo!" Tammy yelled from the bathroom.

I looked at the food I was hungry as hell too, after all that fucking. I grabbed the plate and devoured everything.

Damn shorty could cook. She made me think of Keisha, shit I just thought about it. Keisha hadn't called me in a minute, my suspicions raised.

"I'll get back to that later." I said.

"Come on here and take a shower boy." Tammy yelled.

I got up, sat the plate down, and went in the bathroom.

"Damn girl!" I stated.

"Nigga what?" Tammy asked smiling.

She was ass naked, I know you ain't talkin' 'bout me being naked when you just fucked me last night."

"Nah, you just fine as shit!" I complimented making her smile.

I went ahead and got in the shower, Tammy had just got out, and was now drying off. "So, what's up, you gonna be with me or what Fox?" Tammy questioned.

"Girl, I told you where I stand wit' that. I got a girl and I'm sure your fine ass got a man. Now if I was solo I'd bun you, but right now I can't."

"Well, your key is under the pillow and you're welcomed here anytime."

Damn she won't take no for an answer'. I shook my head as my thoughts roamed.

"And Fox your fine ass is mine now. I don't care who your girl is, but I ain't taking no for an answer." Tammy was persistent and aggressive.

She didn't know, that was my biggest turn on. I couldn't let her know that though. Me and Tammy had sex a couple more times, before I found out, she had a baby father who'd just came home from prison. She wanted to continue, but I stopped it out of respect.

"Muthafucka who is you to tell me I don't need to fuck you anymore?" Tammy yelled. "Nigga you mine! I been informed you on that. I don't care about my baby father's ass. I'll stab your ass."

"What? See, Tammy, you gonna make yourself regret those words if you ever pull out a knife." I warned her. "Tammy look baby girl, you know I fucks wit' you, but we just ain't gonna be fucking like that."

"Damn, I knew I was gonna catch feelings for your ass Fox. I didn't mean too, but I did. You can't say you don't feel nothing for me."

Tammy had started tripping,acting crazy.

"Tammy, I do." I lied because I knew I loved Keisha. "I just didn't know you were still in a relationship with your baby father." Now I flipped it on her.

Tammy looked guilty as hell, "Boo I was going to tell you." Tammy said.

"Baby girl we all right, it's no hard feelings, and I'ma still come to visit."

"Boy you better." Tammy smiled.

I went over and hugged her tight and kissed her forehead as she held me.

"Damn why couldn't things have been different?" Tammy whispered. "I wish I would've met you sooner Fox."

"I know what you mean Tammy." I agreed.In my mind this broad was tripping.

CHAPTER THIRTEEN

I continued to visit Tammy, I frequently ran into her baby's father Eugene. Eugene was a tall, cocky, light-skinned bama from Maryland. I always showed him respect, but he looked like he wanted to trouble. Eugene drove a black Suburban SUV. He thought he was hard coming from the pen, but what he didn't know was that niggas like me didn't even see him. I found out, Eugene had started beating on Tammy. Tammy screamed she was pregnant by me and Eugene kicked her in the stomach. She had to be admitted to the emergency room.

I went to D.C. General hospital to see her, but I wasn't allowed in because I wasn't on the list as immediate family. I walked back downstairs and waited in the lobby of the hospital. While I was waiting, pondering on things, I went to the phone booth and dialed Keisha's number.

"Hello?" Louise answered.

"Keisha back yet, Louise?" I asked.

"Oh, ah, nah baby she still gone."

"Alright, tell her I called and to call me, thank you!"

"Okay, Suga." Louise said.

Keisha hadn't called a nigga or nothing. It had been about three and half weeks now. What the fuck was going on, she knew how important it was for her to let me know she was all right. Shit seemed strange.

All of sudden my money had gone low and she was also gone now. All type of crazy thoughts was running through my head. I walked out the booth and saw a flower vendor. I went and brought a big beautiful bouquet of all types of colorful flowers. I had them delivered to Tammy's room with a note.

I'm sorry to hear of your pain. I wish I could free you of it. I want you to know, I'm wishing you well and keeping you healthy in my thoughts. Call me 397-3014. Fox!

I sent the flowers and caught the bus home, I didn't know if she was really pregnant by me anyway. Later that afternoon, I was sitting on the strip chilling. My beeper went off, I didn't notice the number.

I felt excited, "Damn, it took Keisha long enough to hit a nigga." I said. I was going to cuss her ass out.

"Hey, Sco, let me use your cell phone." I asked.

Sco tossed me his cell phone, I punched the dialed the number then hit the send button.

"Somebody page me?" I asked after hearing someone pick up the phone.

It was quiet for a minute, then I heard a lady crying. I thought Keisha was hurt.

"Baby are you all right?" I asked concerned.

"No, I'm not…all right, I just lost my baby!" The voice cried.

Then I realized it wasn't Keisha, it was Tammy.

"Oh, hi there, little Miss Muffin." I tried to cheer her up.

I heard her laugh through her tears. "That's why I wanted you to be mine Fox. You always made me laugh when I was sad. You always made me feel safe and protected when I was scared. I was scared of Eugene's ass. Damn, Fox I love you so much. I know you told me you got a girl, that made me respect you even more. I want to be your friend 'cause you stuck in my heart." Tammy said.

I sighed, I didn't know what to say. Tammy was good peeps, but I was wit' Keisha. "We straight Tammy, but is it true you were pregnant by me or Eugene?" I asked.

Tammy was silent for a minute. "Hello I'm here." Tammy whispered. "Yes, I was pregnant by you Fox."

I sighed heavily, "Girl why didn't you tell me?"

"Fox because I wanted to get you by yourself. I had fucked Eugene a couple of times but was already pregnant and I only fucked you without a condom on purpose. I didn't know Eugene was coming home so soon."

"Damn bitches treacherous with their shit." I silently mumbled.

"Eugene thought it was his baby until I told him it was yours." Tammy explained.

"Eugene asked me was I going to have it and I told him yeah. Because I wanted your baby. Eugene had been beating on me since he got home. Fox. I thought that would've made him leave for good. But Eugene punched me in my nose, busting it, then he kicked me in my stomach so hard, I vomited up blood.

"My little sister was crying, and the kids were screaming. Eugene continued to bang my head to the floor. I was unconscious, I don't want him around me ever again. Fox, I mean that, I'm thinking about moving. My sister says he keeps coming over, Fox." Tammy said.

Tears started rolling down my eyes as I listened to Tammy. I hadn't even realized tears was coming down my face, when I answered Tammy she could hear the pain in my voice.

"Fox?" Tammy hollered.

"Yeah, I'm here little Miss Muffin."

"Baby I'm so…so sorry." Tammy cried. "I should have told you sooner, maybe we could've prevented this disaster. Fox baby don't cry."

I cried anyway, I wanted a baby and this nigga had killed my only baby. She didn't want to deal with his abusive ass, but she was too scared to tell him the truth.

I didn't appreciate no nigga beating on a broad, but in the hood, you mind ya' own business. That was their affairs, but now it had become my affair because he took it too far.

Plus, he didn't live around my hood, his entry pass was just denied.

"Fox, I'm scared he gonna beat me again." Tammy said.

"Look Little Miss Muffin. You ain't gotta to be scared no more, I got you. You hear me girl!" I asked.

Tammy was crying again. "Yeah."

"That nigga won't be up ya' spot no more. Just hit me when you ready to come home a'ight."

"Okay." Tammy said.

"Thank you, Fox, and I'm sorry again."

"Look you ain't got to apologize sweetheart. I understand the situation. When you have the knowledge to understand situations and people you learn to mature. I don't blame you, you still my Little Miss Muffin."

Tammy laughed, while crying at the same time.

"Boy I wish I could marry your ass. You are so sweet, and th…thank you for all these beautiful flowers." Tammy started crying harder. "Why can't I have you?" She yelled.

"Tammy calm down." I replied. "You still have a piece of me because we still have a friendship as long as we got that, there's still a chance.

"I'ma keep holding on to what you said to Fox. I'm not going to press it, but it makes me feel better knowing it's there. I love you."

"Me too." I answered, as I hung up.

CHAPTER FOURTEEN

"Ha…ha…" Li-Poo laughed. "Y'all niggas crazy."

"Nah nigga you a lunchbox." Tye said. "Squirrel what's up?"

"Ain't shit Young just thinking." I responded.

"Don't trip shorty, I know you want that nigga. We'll get 'em." Sco said.

We were in front of Tammy's building ten deep. Some niggas were hustling, and some were just enjoying the company.

We were on the top steps, it was pitch black dark, on the bottom, it had a light. So, if someone was to come in the building they couldn't see on the top steps, but we could see whoever clear as day.

A couple of days ago I had gone and picked Tammy up from the hospital. Now she was upstairs in her apartment as we were talking, a figure appeared in the front door and stopped. It was Eugene, he had on some faded dark blue jeans, black Timberlands, and a black leather jacket.

He looked up toward the top steps, I knew he stopped because he couldn't see up there where we were. All of us had on Eddie Bauer jumpsuits, army fatigues, with black Eddie Bauer coats. This was our grinding gear and the majority of us was strapped.

Eugene looked around, I told my man Sco and Big Juicy that he couldn't come back to this building or around here. Sco and Big Juicy were big dudes, they were older and had done time down Lorton. One of the most violent state pens in the United States. Eugene wasn't no little dude, he just had come home from Haganstown Maryland pen.

I'd have to kill the bama if I got into a physical altercation with him. So, I sent Sco and Juicy at him.

"Hey, Lova you ain't welcomed around this spot no more, so I advise you to beat ya feet." Sco demanded as he walked down from the top steps.

"What, nah man my baby mama lived upstairs. That's my girl." Eugene replied.

"Nah homes that's our girl." Big Juicy added, as he stepped beside Sco.

Eugene was looking at both of them in defiance. They had on matching Eddie Bauer jumpsuits and black Skully caps.

"We don't allow no dude who don't live around here to beat on our women." Big Juicy said.

"But…" Eugene got cut off quickly.

"But nuthin'." Big Juicy retorted.

"Plus, you killed my young nigga baby." Sco snapped. "You lucky yo' ass didn't go back to prison. My young nigga hated that tho. Nuff talk speed on before ya get peed on." Sco threatened.

"And when I piss I don't miss." Big Juicy also threatened.

Me and Li-Poo came down the steps laughing. Eugene stared at me, with pure hatred in his eyes.

"Slim I advise you to get to stepping. The call was made now answer it." I said.

"Nigga what, that's my bitch upstairs!" Eugene yelled.

"Gene you better pump ya brakes slim before I crash you. I'm giving you the opportunity to bounce. Don't gas yourself up. I'm sensing a lot of disrespect and hostility coming from you. Just roll and don't come back. If you ever come back or think about beating Tammy again, we gonna beat you like you stole something. Now kick rocks." I warned sternly.

Eugene still tried to protest, "That's my baby up there. How you gonna stop a man from seeing his child?"

"Man, fuck dis shit." Sco said pissed.

"Gene you about to get a thirty-minute workout." I said. "My mans and 'em ain't trying to hear that shit. You should have thought about that when you were beating Tammy's ass." I told him.

Eugene got defiant and tried to walk up the steps. Before I knew it, I threw two straight jabs and punched him in his face. My one two usually knocked a nigga ass out, but Eugene just had a busted nose and lip.

It looked like my punches didn't faze him. Eugene lunged for me and it was on. Li-Poo surprised the shit out of me when he started throwing multiple blows to Eugene's face and head. Sco grabbed Eugene from the back in the full Nelson and Big Juicy started throwing heavy blows to Eugene's body. The jump was on, niggas started running down the steps to get part of the action.

Sco, had let Eugene drop to the ground. We had beat him unconscious. Blood was all over the hallway. Tammy appeared at the top of the steps. I ran to the top of the steps while Li-Poo, Sco, Big Juicy, and the rest of the mob was still whupping Eugene's ass.

"Baby girl go back in the house." I instructed her.

Tammy was silently crying, "No, boo I want to see that nigga ass get beat the way he beat me." Tammy said.

"Tammy…listen it's gonna get worse." I told her.

"So, what I don't care, that nigga beat me senseless for years." Tammy insisted.

"A'ight suit yourself, but don't get to bitchin' or hollering about don't kill him." I told her.

"I wouldn't give a fuck if y'all kill him. He killed our baby." Tammy insisted.

"A'ight now." I said as I went to get back into the action.

Eugene's head was lying against the steel door frame when I came back down the steps. His face was swollen beyond recognition. I took my Timberland boot and kicked his head against the door frame.

Eugene's head hit the door frame with a loud thud. Blood poured out the back of Eugene's head and blood was running out of his mouth. When Tammy saw the way, I kicked him she cringed. Somebody had given this crazy ass nigga Tye a baseball bat.

Tye walked up and began beating Eugene's arms and legs.

"Nah, Joe give me that bat." Big Juicy said. "If you trying to break his arms and legs, you gotta swing it a certain kinda way."

Tye handed Juicy the bat, Juicy swung that joint like a professional baseball player.

CRACK… was the sound Eugene's bones made as Big Juicy hit Eugene in the middle of each arms.

"Them bad boys definitely broken." Juicy said.

Then he swung again and again breaking both Eugene's legs and ankles. Eugene just laid there between the door frame unconscious and bleeding profusely.

"Is he dead?" Tye asked.

"Not yet." I answered, pulling out my Glock.

"Noooo…!" Everybody yelled simultaneously.

"Put ya hamma up young. This joker is out of it, he won't be back around this joint, let his ass suffer." Sco advised.

"Yeah you'd be doing him a favor by killing him." Juicy added.

I put my hamma back up.

"A'ight strip this nigga ass naked." Boo-Boo suggested.

Everybody looked at Boo-Boo confused, but I walked over to Eugene anyway and started taking off his boots and socks. Everybody else joined in and took off his clothes, until Eugene was completely naked.

"Hey Ronald, go get that gas can outta my car trunk." Sco ordered.

"Damn Joe, I thought you wasn't going to kill him." I reminded.

"Nah, we gonna burn up all his clothes." Sco replied.

"Oh a'ight." I nodded.

Juicy dragged Eugene's body by the cut and left him there. Ronald came back with a big red and yellow gas can. He handed it to Sco.

Sco dumped the gas on the pile of Eugene's clothes and lit a match. The clothes immediately went up in flames.

"A'ight everybody let's roll." Sco said.

As me and Li-Poo was exiting the hallway, I noticed three figures dressed in all black creeping on the side building. I thought it was hands-up, I grabbed my .40. I was going to punish these bamas, then I saw the reflector bands on their arms that said Police.

Ooh shit! That ain't hands-up, them track stars trying to creep. I thought. "Track stars...track stars...track stars!" I yelled out as me and Li-Poo broke into a sprint.

I jammed my .40 back into my side pocket and hauled ass like a rabbit getting chased by a fox. Niggas took off running every way. The jump-outs didn't know where to run or who to chase.

I was running fast as a Nascar car, when I looked beside me Li-Poo must had kicked in some turbo because this bama flew past me, fast as a muthafucka. I looked back to see that a track star was on my ass and gaining. This muthafucka ran like Robocop, now I see why Li-Poo hit turbo.

I bent the corner and ran down towards the one hundred steps. The hundred steps were the long steps around Lincoln Heights that leads you from the Maze to the bottom of the Valley.

These steps were famous in the hood because if you were familiar with them, like I was, you could never get caught if the police were chasing you. You could run at the top of the steps and jump, the momentum of your body weight would push you through the air and you'd glide in the air, clearing about rows of steps.

However, if you weren't experienced or careful when you jumped. Your landing could prove to be disastrous. You would most likely fall and bust your head or break your foot and or ankles. I was very well experienced at these steps. As a kid when I first moved around Lincoln Heights I used to jump them for fun, believing I could fly.

I only fell once and that was because ice was on the third row of the steps. Luckily snow cushioned my fall, I saw dudes lose all their front teeth, get their heads busted, legs broke, and more trying to clear the jump.

I peeped back at the Robocop he was still on my ass. I hopped a wall by the last cut before I reached the hundred steps. Robocop cleared the wall like a track hurdle. That's why they call the jump-outs track stars.

They were fast and agile, and they ran like they were Maurice Green or somebody. I cleared the first row of steps. Robocop was right behind me; the hundred steps was next. I speeded up and jumped, I loved the feeling as I extended my arms like wings, just gliding through the air.

I landed a perfect ten on the fourth row. I ran and leaped again to clear the next four rows. As I landed another perfect ten, I heard a loud 'Thump', then the rails on the steps vibrated hard. I looked back and saw Robocop tumbling down the steps like a rag doll.

His arms were flailing wilding everywhere and his legs were twisted all kinds of ways in the air. His walkie talkie went crashing to the ground into pieces. I cleared all the steps and stopped, I looked back, Robocop was out of it. I was tempted to go back up there and kill him, but I pushed the thought away.

He had been so pressed to catch me that he didn't know where I was leading his dumbass too. I heard sirens in the distance, I turned around and jogged across the street into the valley.

"What happened Joe?" Fat Tony from the valley asked me.

"I just shook the jump-outs Young as I entered the valley cut. I left one on the hundred steps."

"Let me guess his dumb ass tried to follow you and jumped the steps?" Tony said.

"Yep, bama got twisted too." I replied out of breath.

"You wanna hit this?" Tony asked extending a blunt.

"Nah, I'm straight young."

Tony had been in the cut with Toray and his brother Greg smoking weed. I told them about us whupping Eugene and burning his clothes before the jumps-out came out of nowhere creeping. They didn't know about us beating Eugene's ass. It was just a coincidence.

I didn't know where Li-Poo ass had run, but from the way his ass ran, I knew he had gotten away.

CHAPTER FIFTEEN

My pockets was hurting and I needed some real money. Five hundred dollars wasn't no money. That was chump change, compared to what I'm used to having.

Li-Poo had gotten away from the track stars just like I thought. He had stayed up my house, a nigga pockets were hungry, and they needed to be fed. I heard about a big dice game going on down on fifth street alley.

That was the same alley that Mohammad shot at me in. I figured maybe I could catch his ass down there and flat line him. I needed something big in case we got into a shootout or something. I told Li-Poo, we were going on a caper.

"Shid... a'ight joe." Li-Poo said. He acted like he was all for it.

I went in the house, went into my stash spot, and grabbed a Tech-9 with a thirty-two shot clip and a Smith and Wesson 9mm for Li-Poo. I went under my bed in the far corner and grabbed my vest. I strapped it on and pulled my black Hugo Boss sweat shirt over top of it. I came back outside, and Li-Poo was on the front porch of my building waiting for me. I called him in the hallway.

"Here." I handed him the Smith and Wesson.

He looked kinda awkward with the gun.

"You know how to use that?" I asked.

"Yeah."

To my surprise he flicked the safety on and off to prove, he knew a little some 'em, some 'em.

"Follow me." I instructed.

We took the back streets towards the alley. Once we were in the middle section of the street, we decided to cut between the houses. I knew that the niggas probably had a look-out, so I took a short cut. We went through the houses and stepped behind the alley. To my surprise there wasn't any look-outs.

The sky was beginning to fade dark blue, it was about to be nighttime in thirty or forty minutes.

I slid my mask on, "Put your mask on nigga." I ordered Li-Poo.

"I don't have one." He said.

Damn I forgot who I was with. He wasn't used to this type of shit. I pulled out a black bandanna that I always kept on me and handed it to him.

"Wrap that around your face." I whispered.

Li-Poo wrapped the bandanna around his face and pulled his Skully hat low.

"A'ight joe, let's roll." I pulled the Tech, out of the leather book bag I had brought it in.

Li-Poo pulled out the Smith and Wesson .9mm and we started creeping.

"Back doe little joe. Come on Love! Break this Nigga!" I heard as dice cackled on the ground.

I turned back to Li-Poo and put my finger to my lips. I had gone over the routine as we walked down here.

"When I get in the alley where the gambling spot at just cover me." I told Li-Poo. "Make sure nobody try to run."

"Got you cuz." Li-Poo agreed.

As I entered the spot, I peeped in, for real I was looking for two niggas. Mohammad and Hairio. I scanned the area twice and didn't see them.

"Shit they not here." I grumbled.

But a gang of other niggas that hang down there was, and the pot on the ground was big. It looked like at least nine thousand dollars. Not including all the niggas standing around with stacks of money in their hands.

Once I looked around, I realized, this little back cut was a death trap. Now I was on the outside looking in. It was built like a cubicle, it was one way in and one way out. There was a gate on one side of the cubicle, but by the time you tried to hop that joint a nigga would be done shot you off that bitch.

"I used to be down here gambling all the time." I said to myself.

I looked back at Li-Poo and signaled, I was going in.

"Hands up and faces to the ground! Y'all know what time it is!" I yelled as I entered the spot.

The Tech-9 had a nasty muzzle that made niggas want to shit on themselves. J-Bo was Li-Poo code name I had given him.

"J-Bo make sure no muthafuckin' body even wiggle. If so blow, they muthafuckin' brains out. We ain't come here to play we came to collect bills. All muthafuckin' car keys in front of you!" I continued yelling. "If I find any house, car, or any type of key somebody getting shot tonight."

Niggas threw their car and house keys in front of them.

"A'ight now stay face down." I ordered. "We can do this the easy way or the hard way. Anybody who play hero gettin' shot to a zero by J-Bo." I looked up and Li-Poo was gone. "What the fuck!" I grumbled under my breath.

This bama left me. I kept talking, acting as if he was there. "Watch' em if they try to cuff any money, J-Bo." I said.

Niggas were stiff as mannequins. I went around shaking down every nigga in attendance. As I was shaking them down, I was collecting the money putting it in my black leather book bag. I took all the car keys and every pair of shoes and socks the niggas had on.

I tied all the shoestrings in a knot and threw them up on a power line. I did this just in case one of them tried to chase me. This alley had so many broken glass bottles and rocks, it was guaranteed for them to cut their feet up. Shit even just walking with socks on it was a guarantee, they'd cut their feet.

After I had collected everything, I started to back out of the cubicle.

"Come on J-Bo." I said, pretending Li-Poo was still there with me.

I heard one of the dudes on the ground whisper furiously. "No!"

"Thank you for yo…" I was cut off by the sudden movement of a dark-skinned dude who jumped and bolted near the fence near the far corner of the cubicle.

Instantly my trigger finger reacted, *Flop…Flop…Flop…Flop.* The Tech spit, four bullets slammed into his back. He dropped instantly three steps away from the fence. He must've a gun over there.

"Any other muthafuckin' volunteers?" I hollered.

Everybody remained stiff, I peaked at the dude who tried to bolt. He was lying on his stomach head turned to the side, taking deep, slow breaths. The bottom of his feet was bleeding from the glass on the ground. As I started to retreat again, with the money in the book bag. I heard a dude furiously mumbling under his breath,

"I told 'em…I told his dumb ass!"

I slid back through the houses and ran like the track stars was on my back. I didn't stop running until I hit 50th street around Lincoln Heights. I had put the Tech back in the book bag and slung it over my shoulder. I walked the back way through the cut to my building.

"What's up Squirrel?"

"Ain't shit Dorothy." I answered.

"You see Sco?" She asked.

"Nah I'm just coming from over my folk's house." I answered.

"Oh, okay." Dorothy was Sco's woman.

She was brown-skinned with a cute face and phat to death.

I calmly walked to my building and went into the house. Big Doris room door was shut. I figured her, and Mickey were in there. I went to my room, closed the door, and locked it. I cut my lamp on and dumped the money on the table.

"Chi-Ching…damn I hit payday." I said excited.

I heard sirens and fire trucks in the distance outside my window. I already knew what that was all about. I counted all the money. I couldn't believe I had at least twenty-thousand, nine hundred, ninety dollars and sixty cents.

"Damn Joe, I struck payday. Being hands-up for today wasn't bad." I told myself.

I counted the money again just to make sure I wasn't lunching. It was accurate.

"Fuck that, I'm putting this in my stash. I'ma buy me a nice car though." I said.

I had a new stash spot now, I had neatly cut a hole in the wall behind my dresser, big enough to fit the black metal box I got from the vendor stand caper.

I had it were you can fix it back in place with a little crazy glue. You would never be able to tell it was there. Plus, my big heavy dresser was blocking it. You had to strain with most of your strength to be able to move that big boy. I put the money up and pushed the heavy dresser back in place.

I was back on, I had been wondering what happened to Li-Poo ass when my beeper started vibrating. I picked up the phone and dialed the number back.

"Hello somebo…"

"Joe, you a'ight?" Li-Poo asked cutting me off.

"Man, where the fuck you at nigga? I barked angrily.

"I'm at home." He replied.

"Home! How the fuck did you get home?"

"I caught a ride wit' this dude I know."

"Get the fuck outta here, you welling like shit!" I told him. "Why did you leave me, Young? I can't believe you rolled out on me like that? Anything could have happened to me!"

"Joe, I'am be real, I got paranoid." Li-Poo said.

"Paranoid!" I repeated. "Oh yeah, it's cool young I ain't even tripping for real." I was mad as hell, but I had to maintain my composure. "Hey Li-Poo where that joint at?"

"Ooh it's outside of your building. Look out your window and look for a green sour cream and onion tater chip bag."

"What you actually left that joint out like that?" I asked. "Anything could have happened to that joint in that spot. When the jump-outs, jump-out the first spot they check, is potato chip bags for stashes. When pipe heads start geeking they search every bag on the fuckin' ground. Man hold on!" I said.

I lifted my room window and didn't see no green potato chip bag because it had gotten dark. There were some lights out there, but not directly shinning in this particular area. I was hoping nobody didn't find that hamma. That was a vicious come up. I definitely didn't want to deal wit' Snuk.

These were all his guns really. I was just babysitting them. If I needed to use them, then I could. I only had two Glock .40s, a Mac-11, a .380, and a .25 caliber. The rest of the hammas was Snuk's.

I grabbed my big heavy-duty flash light and went outside. I didn't give a fuck if Li-Poo was still on the phone or not. This absentminded ass nigga, I'm glad his ass did run because if he would have seen me shoot that dude he probably would have went beserk. No telling what he would have done. I walked outside and flashed the flashlight around. I spotted the green chip bag, grabbed it, and looked inside. The hamma was in there, I sighed with relief. I went back upstairs to my room.

"Hello."

"Yeah, you find it?" Li-Poo was still on the phone.

"Yeah young."

"So, how much did we get?" Li-Poo asked.

'We this muthafucka buggin'.' I thought. "Nuthin!" I lied.

"Nothing?" Li-Poo asked in disbelief.

"Nah nuthin' nigga. When you left me I had to get the fuck up outta that joint. They had a rack of loot down that joint too. If you would have stayed, we would've came off."

"Maan damn!" Li-Poo grumbled.

"Joe I'm about to bounce, I'll holla at you later." I told Li-Poo.

"A'ight cuz I'll see ya later."

I hung up. Li-Poo didn't know that I wasn't ever going to take him on another caper. He lucky he was my cousin. My family didn't know I was doing dirt and shooting people. But if he wasn't family I probably would have shot his ass. In my world you never go on a mission wit' a coward 'cause they'll always fail you.

CHAPTER SIXTEEN

"Excuse me girlfriend can I get five minutes of your time." I asked this beautiful light brown-skinned, short, curly haired female. She as about 5'8, sexy as silk sheets.

She had on a body hugging, white and blue long summer dress, opened toe heels, and everyone of her sexy toes was painted red. Damn she was sexy, she was in the carry out called the Shrimp Boat, on Benning Road northeast, East Capitol Street.

I had come back from Ridge Road Southeast, and walked up there to clear my mind. Also, to see if Keisha was home. She wasn't, I was curious about the grandmother helping shit. I felt as though she'd abandoned me. I decided to move forward. No use in prolonging, it had been damn near two months since I'd heard from her.

My heart was worried and hurting. Louise didn't seem too concerned, it was either the crack or she knew Keisha was well. Which meant Keisha was up to no good.

"Who me?" The beautiful woman responded.

"Yeah, you beautiful. You're the only star that's shining in here."

She smiled. She was accompanied by three of her girlfriends, who were also dressed to impress. She excused herself from her friends and stepped forward.

I noticed the grimaces on her friends faces, when they looked at me. I wasn't dressed to impress. I had on some army fatigues, a black T-shirt, and black Timberland boots. My black Skully was pulled down, this was my block grinding gear. They certainly didn't approve of it, neither did she from the hesitation in her steps, I caught on quick.

"Hi...hi, what's up?" She asked.

"Girlfriend I assure you, I'm no thief. I just fell on hard times recently, I'm in the process of getting myself back together. Right now, I'm dealing with a case of a broken heart and I think you can put it back together."

I noticed a smile had crept in the corners of her mouth. Her friends glanced our way.

"Um…you all right, but you not my type." She said.

"Hold up excuse my manners, what's your name beautiful." I ignored her comment about not being her type.

"My name is Michelle, but my friends call me Chelle."

"Okay, my friends call me Fox, now that we've been properly introduced, let's start over."

"Like I said in the beginning if you were paying attention, you not my type, plus you too short." She said again.

Her friends were in earshot and busted out laughing.

"What, nah Ms. Chelle I know you not trying to clown a nigga cause of my attire."

"Oh yeah, you can do something with that too, you look like a thugga."

She pronounced thug like a white girl, with the roll of her tongue. Her friends were cracking up, she was straight dissing me.

One of her girlfriends hollered. "Come on girl, he broke as glass and he riding them Timbs like he pushing something big."

All the girls broke out in laughter. I wanted to kirk out on them, but I was in no mood. My charm didn't work on this bun-bun.

"Buy me a happy meal." Another one of the girls hollered.

More laughter followed, I had to laugh at that one myself. Chelle stepped off back to her crowd of girlfriends. Her rejection added to my sunken mood. I didn't show it though.

"Y'all ladies enjoy y'all selves." I said as I exited the Shrimp Boat.

"Yeah when can you pay for it?" Another one of the girls shot back.

Again, they were cracking up laughing. I peaked at Chelle and smirked. She stared and laughed. No hard feelings, nothing beats a failure as long as you try. I walked all the way back to my hood Lincoln Heights and sat on the wall. Mostly everybody was gone, doing their own thang.

Pipe head Pet walked over to me. "Hey baby."

"What's happening Pet?" I asked.

"Ain't shit." She said in her New York accent.

I loved to hear Pet talk, for her to be a pipe head she was sharp as a whip and smart.

"Let me do your hair tonight." She requested.

"I'll think about it, I might have some plans. If I don't I'll be up ya' spot." I told her.

"Okay baby."

"Oh, don't forget to bring your two little boys over so I can cut their hair for school next week." I reminded her.

"I won't." Pet replied.

"A'ight call us even then."

Pet smiled, I always took care of my neighborhood youngstas. I used to cut the little boys hair in the hood just to keep their appearance up.

Because some of the mothers were so strung out on crack that they didn't care how their kids looked. People watched out for me, when I was that age, so that was my way of repaying them. It was to help somebody else in need. It made me feel good too.

"Squirrel." Pet said. "A dude came through here looking for you in a blue car.

He said he been trying to catch you and he'll be back. I don't want you getting shot at again, so you be careful baby. You holding?" Pet asked worriedly.

I lifted my shirt and showed her two massive Glock .40s. "In guns I trust." I replied.

Pet nodded and headed back across the street to her apartment building. "Don't forget your hair boy!" She yelled.

"I won't!" I yelled back.

I already knew who she was talking about. It was my man Sandman. He'd been trying to catch me for the longest. We just kept missing each other.

I thought about how the pretty broad Chelle blew me off today. That jive bruised my ego. I was already down, I day dreamed about us just chilling together. Me massaging those pretty feet, kissing those thigh soft lips…

"Hey youngin'!" A voice broke my train of thoughts.

I immediately fell back over the wall and grabbed my hamma. I wasn't going to look in case somebody tried to me a move.

"Nah youngsta it's me Sandman." I peeked across the street and there he was sitting in his blue '92' Maxima.

I got up, put my gun back up, and walked across the street to the car. Sandman was sitting behind the wheel in a grey Versace silk shirt, Armani linen pants, and some soft crush slippers. Sandman was killin' 'em softly.

"What's up nigga?" He greeted me with a big smile. "Nigga your ass is elusive as a cat. Where you been youngin? I heard you did a little stretch in Oak Hill." He said.

"Yeah I had to put them hot rocks in a nigga ass." I replied.

Sandman smiled with pride, "That's my nigga." He said. "I also hear you got beef in three directions."

"Yeah don't worry I can handle that." I assured. "I'm just trying to get back on my feet."

"That's why I came to see you. I got something decent for you. Let's ride." He instructed.

"Lead the way." I said.

"Youngin' you did one helluva job on Ted."

I thought Sandman was going to be mad that I somewhat over did it. My heart was pumping fast and I was afraid to speak because he might detect it.

"Shorty man…you a muthafucka wit' your shit. I fucks wit' you all the way live. My hands are your hands. Anything you need you got. That was gangsta how you put that work in. Damn youngin' you shot him in the face without killing him. Woo-wee…I love that gangsta shit." Sandman boasted excitedly.

I couldn't believe it, he approved of my work. This nigga was more vicious than I thought. Well…he had to be vicious from the jump in order to put a hit on his own blood, but hey his blood violated and that's how the game goes.

"Lil' Fox I got something for you. Reach underneath your seat and grab that bag." He said.

I reached under my seat and grabbed the black miniature duffle bag.

"Open it." He said.

I opened the bag and saw a large stack of money.

"That's fifteen thousand dollars. The five G's I owe you and an extra ten g's as a bonus for your good service." Sandman said.

I was happy as a muthafucka, I was back on now.

"Youngin' listen I need a soldier like you on my team. It ain't too many youngin's out here like you. If you fuck wit' me, you'll see money like you want too. Plus, the side missions will be extra profit in your pocket. I'm about to break out with some good dope on the avenue. Just me and you can set up shop and work.

I already got my hand down there, so it won't be no drama setting up shop, and you ain't gotta worry it'll already be bagged up in bundles. Our rule is we only work from six a.m to twelve p.m.

On Friday from nine a.m to two p.m. No if, ands, or buts…we gotta be strict youngin'. If they come one minute late don't serve 'em. No sales and I mean no sales, after that time. I don't care if they bring a thousand dollars. You hear me?" Sandman said.

"Yeah." I said. I had accepted his offer, but I had a good feel for this.

"Peep this at exactly two o-clock we shut down shop, if the fiends want to buy my dope they'll be their ass there on time. Ya dig." Sandman continued.

"Yeah, that sounds proper." I said.

"So, is you wit' me?" He asked.

"Yeah I'm definitely wit' you." I replied.

"A'ight then let's get this money." He said.

"Where we cruising too?" I asked Sandman.

"Oh, I gotta make a political move out Blue Plains Motors in VA. I got a man I need to holla at. Just chill shorty, you wit' me today." Sandman responded.

I laid back and closed my eyes. Sandman turned on his CD player to the sounds of Curtis Mayfield and the Impressions.

"Now that's my type of music." I said.

"Boy whatcha know about that youngin'?" He asked.

I began singing along with the lyrics to the song… "Man, oh man…in the middle of France…though odds was against us…we still took our chance."

Sandman smiled, "Youngsta you know what you know."

We drove up in the Nissan dealership and parked in the back.

"Come on young nigga." Sandman said as he turned off the ignition and got out.

We walked to this large white building, which was the car dealership's main office. As we approached the door a Spanish dude greeted us.

"Hey, Sandman." He spoke in a light Spanish accent.

Sandman greeted him in return then introduced us.

"Jose this my youngin' Lil' Fox. Shorty on the come up like us."

I was slightly thrown off guard for a second, but then I caught on to what Sandman had said.

"Make yourself at home." The Spanish dude said. "If you want something to eat there's plenty of food in the fridge back that way." He pointed to the back hall.

"I appreciate it." I told him.

I peeped that they were about to conduct some business, so I excused myself. I told them I was going to walk around the car lot. Sandman and Jose smiled. I didn't know if that was for me being respectful or what, but it seemed like a good sign.

"Yes, please do excuse us, we have some old times to catch up on. I did ten years in the Feds with my man Sandman here." He extended his hand and I gave him a nice firm shake.

After that him and Sandman headed toward the back office.

I walked outside and walked along the line of parked cars for sale. There were a lot of nice cars, old to new Maximas, 280Zs, 88 anniversaries 300Zs, Altimas, Nissan Sentras, and more.

As I was coming around the line of cars to head back into the building. I saw a line of 92 300 Turbo ZXs. Them joints were pretty.

I imagined pushing one, flexing around my hood. I'd be done really stepped my game up.

I thought about buying it, but I wanted to stay low key. The price tag read twenty-two thousand, three hundred dollars even. I knew I could get that joint, I tried the door handle, and the door came open. I sat down in the bucket seats and envisioned myself driving it.

Knock...knock...knock...

Jose scared the shit out of me as he knocked on the window.

"You like?" He asked.

"Yeah, but my pockets ain't this deep right now lova."

"How much you got?" He asked. "Just give me twenty g's for it and you can be adios amigo." Jose said smiling.

"I can only get 'round bout fifteen." I said.

"Cash?"

"Yeah!"

"Deal." He agreed. "Keep the five g's as a gift for being Sandman's youngsta."

"What!" I couldn't believe it.

"I'll vouch for the licenses and insurance Jose." Sandman said as he walked up.

"Alrighty then, deals made." Jose said happily.

Jose had just fast talked a nigga. He definitely was business man.

"Look youngin' that's what I'm talkin' bout. Step that shit up." Sandman boasted enthusiastically. "You only live once, now go get your money." Sandman emphasized.

I realized Sandman didn't say he'd pay for it. He simply said he'd vouch for the insurance and license, since I was too young to come off the lot with this.

I went and got my money, I handed it to Sandman. Sandman took the money to Jose, they came back a moment later smiling. Jose threw me the car keys and the title to the car. It was in Sandman's alias name, John. I couldn't pronounce the last name. Sandman winked at me, both men embraced each other and said their farewells as we departed.

"A'ight Jose nice meeting you again." I said when I got in the car.

I had already pictured how I was going to customize it. Rims, tinted windows, a big stereo system, and more. I started the engine and pressed the gas pedal. The engine roared, Sandman walked up to my driver's side window.

"Yougin' this one on me. We watched you from the window, I knew you wanted something fly, that's why I brought you out here. Heard 'bout you burnin' ya Caddy. This should make up for that. But be ever mindful to save your money, cause if you get caught up. I'm not your lawyer. Feel me? I just came home, so I'ma keep it real wit' cha. Save your money, my money ain't your money. Your money is your money."

I had to respect that, it's a part of the game. We drove off the parking lot, I followed Sandman home on the highway.

CHAPTER SEVENTEEN

On our drive back, I was comfortably seated in my new Turbo 300ZX bucket seats. I thought about what Sandman told me.

"This on me." His voice repeated in my head.

The car was actually a gift form him for the work I had put down on his brother.

Sandman was actually testing me to see how I was going to handle money. "Sly muthafucka." I said.

Upon arriving back to the hood, I drove up the block looking sweet. I saw my man Pee-Wee standing on Lincoln Heights basketball court. I drove pass in slow motion. Pee-Wee was looking at me, mouthing words in slow motion.

"That you Squirrel?"

I threw the peace sign up and hit the gas. Everything sped back up as the Z speeded up quick. I pulled up on my block, people were out there enjoying the day. Sandman, drove up beside me as I parked.

"Yougin' I got some business to attend to, so I'ma head out. I'll hit you on the hip soon, be ready. Shorty be careful, and don't be driving ya car all crazy." Sandman warned. "Remember what I said, your shit is yours not mine, so if you fuck it up, that's on you...you hear me." He asked.

"Yeah, I hear you, Joe. I ain't gonna fuck this up." I swore.

"Alright now, I'll holla at cha later." Sandman said and drove off.

As soon as he left, I was excited as hell. I jumped back in my new Z and took a joy ride. Driving myself around show boatin' felt good. I took the Z on dead back streets and gunned the engine. It felt powerful and was quick. I drove back up my hood to the basketball court. Pee-Wee was still out there with some more youngins.

Loc, Buggs, Fruit, Moe, Tye, Adrain, Ramon, and more. They were deep when I pulled up, that made my day. I parked right in the parking lot beside the basketball court.

A few broads were in front of buildings conversating. When they saw me all of them silently watched my approach over to the fellas. I acted like it was just another day. I knew the fellas was gonna interrogate me. I walked up and embraced Pee-Wee and gave out daps.

"What's up y'all?" I asked.

"Same shit…"

"Nothin'…"

"Just chillin'…"

"Hustlin'…"

Were their responses.

"Squirrel, who joint you pushin' your brothers?" Pee-Wee asked.

"Aaah shit…here we go!" I said. "Nah, Joe."

"What that joint stolen? Let me drive that joint." Pee-Wee said.

"Nah, Joe that's my joint. I just bought it, can't you see the paper tags?" I responded.

"Oh, nah let's get that screwdriver out yo' back pocket." Adrian joked.

Everybody busted out laughing. Adrian and Ramon was two red muthafuckas in the hood, they were natural comedians. They were always on joke time…a.k.a J.T. time.

Everybody loved them because they brought humor to any situation just like my man Tye.

"You for real young?" Pee-Wee asked amazed. "I gotta step my hustle game up. Lil' Anthony in the circle still pushing the Benz joint. Omar pushing that New Sho Taurus wagon. Shit everybody stepping it up!" Pee-Wee complained. "I'm still pushing the cinnamon biscuit." Nigga busted out laughing.

We got a hood tradition where we named our hoopties. Pee-Wee had a brown Caprice classic that was fast as a muthafucka.

Pee-Wee was trying to step it up, but couldn't because he was a ladies man, which meant he spent most of his money partying, buying clothes, and weed. He always kept enough money for gas, outfits, and weed.

Unlike Adrian and Ramon who just hustled to buy weed. Those two right there were straight weed heads.

"Hey y'all I'm 'bout to go up E Street and get some smoke." Fruit said.

Fruit was a brown-skinned hustler who loved to go to Go-Gos and fight. Fruit was also a fly dressing nigga.

"Who got ten on it?" Fruit asked.

"Damn Joe, what happened to three or five dollars?" Ramon asked.

Niggas started laughing.

"You know I wanna smoke, but you hurting a brother. They call me Bob now." Ramon said.

"That's a stupid ass name," Fruit replied with a serious look.

"Because Joe, I'm a baller on a budget." Ramon responded.

"Ha...ha...ha!" laughter broke out between everybody.

"That's a funny muthafucka." Pee-Wee said through tears of laughter.

I just shook my head laughing, these was some funny dudes.

"A'ight y'all donations please." Fruit continued asking. "Climb up in grandma Ma and we gone."

Grandma Ma was the name of Fruits big old school limousine Cadillac. It was light grey, with tinted windows. Everybody put in and Fruit, Adrian, Ramon, Loc, Bugg, and Moe piled into the car and drove off. Me, Tye, and Pee-Wee stayed outside kicking it. We walked a few steps to the building front. Tye sat on the wall, while me and Pee-Wee reminisced about when we were kids.

Pee-Wee was like the fourth buddy I met after moving around Lincoln Heights. We met in our second-grade teacher Ms. Wade's class. Me and Pee-Wee bonded naturally because we were both mischievous. We were the class clowns, we'd sneak straws back from lunch and spit, spit balls while Ms. Wade's back was turned.

"That one hit Tisha in the neck." I whispered to Pee-Wee.

We'd burst out in little giggles.

"Alright your turn young." I'd whisper to Pee-Wee.

'Achew...achew'. A big ass spit ball smacked the shit out of a classmate named Sam. Sam was Roman's brother and he was kind of slow.

I died laughing as Sam hollered. "I been hit...I'm hit...I'm going down! Help, Ms. Wade!"

I put my head in the desk and cracked up. Pee-Wee was damn near on the floor laughing. As soon as Ms. Wade turned around we'd straighten up as if nothing happened.

"Who did it Sam?" Ms. Wade asked.

Sam looked around the class, me and Pee-Wee both looked at him and gave him the look like if you tell we gonna jump you after school.

"Damn sure 'nough it was Joseph Johnson!" He screamed. The spit ball was still stuck in Sam's hair.

I couldn't help it, I busted out laughing.

"Joseph go to the principal's office now." Ms. Wade said.

"But...but...he didn't see me do nothing!" Pee-Wee protested.

"Now I said!" Ms. Wade hollered.

Then she cut her eyes at me. I pretended to do my work.

"You're next Jonathan! You think you slick." She said.

I ignored her, Pee-Wee looked like a said puppy leaving the classroom. At 3:00 p.m. class was over, I waited at the corner for Sam. I had to go get him for snitching on Pee-Wee. He came by like the shit ain't never happen. I punched his ass, his big stupid face was hard. He started a goofy run. I tripped him and started to punch him in his face. When I saw him bleeding I let up, he was crying, for some reason I felt sorry for him. So, I kicked him and ran, now he knew not to tattle again.

After that me and Pee-Wee was into everything except the right thing. We used to get in trouble at school, Pee-Wee's mother would whip his ass and mine. That's how I met Ms. Claudette, Pee-Wee's mother. She was like a mother to me also. She'd let me spend the night over Pee-Wee's house. I used to ride my bike every day pass Pee-Wee's house.

Ms. Claudette would call me, "Jonathan."

"Yes ma'am?" I'd answer.

"You hungry? Come on in here and eat." She'd say. Then she'd fix me fried ham, bologna, and cheese, with orange juice every time.

As I got older and was in the streets she'd still fix me the same meal. It was my favorite. I remember one time I spent the night over Pee-Wee's house.

I was supposed to help his family spring clean. Pee-Wee had every damn toy a kid could dream of. His mother and father spoiled him. After everything was done, it was time to leave.

"Let me walk you to the door young." Pee-Wee said.

As we walked to the door a G.I. Joe toy man fell from my pants leg.

"Man, what da… let me pat you down young." Pee-Wee said.

He lifted my pants leg and a whole army of G.I. Joe men fell out.

"Aw shucks." Pee-Wee sighed.

I was embarrassed. As I was cleaning I'd found a toy chest in Pee-Wee's closet, that had been there for I don't how long. His mother wanted everything thrown out, so I helped myself to the G.I. Joe men for my collection. I told Pee-Wee this, and he laughed.

"You can have them Young." He told me. "I don't play wit' em no mo' anyway."

I was relieved. Telling those stories again always made us laugh. Me, Pee-Wee, and Tye was cracking up at the things we had done. I was now fourteen, Pee-Wee was fourteen, and Tye was sixteen, we were all still young. Fruit and the fellas pulled up.

"Who got da lidda light?" Fruit was singing. "Let's smoke y'all."

As soon as we lit the blunts, broads started poppin' up like popcorn. First it was cut lip Boo, then pretty eyes Tiffany, the short Nikki, then Meek-Meek, then the girl who blew me off at the Shrimp Boat carry-out. She looked at me, then joined the crowd of females trying to fill their lungs with free smoke. It was like these bitches had a homing device for weed.

They were nowhere to be found all day. Now they wanted to bring their free loading asses around. I had to admit Chelle looked so good. She had on a white blossom flower shirt exposing her voluptuous cleavage, some tight fitting black jeans, and some open toe heels showing those sexy ass toes. Her hair was cut short and naturally dark, thick, and curly. She looked as if she was mixed.

"Fuck this, somebody fuckin', y'all bitches ain't smoking our shit for free. I put in the pot too, I work hard for the money baby. I can't afford for y'all to smoke off me." Adrian was preaching, he was high as a kite, laughing like a muthafucka.

It was so funny because he was dead serious.

"So, who fucking?" Adrian asked.

Neither girl answered, the blunt was about to be passed to pretty eye Tiffany. As soon as she was bringing it to her lips, Adrian snatched the blunt.

"Bitch I mean what I said. Everybody who ain't fuckin' disappear!" Adrian ordered.

Niggas was cracking up, everybody knew it was gonna be some fuckin' so niggas weren't tripping. Somebody had put a big speaker in the window and played a junkyard Go-Go tape. That seemed to live everything up as Adrian started doing his wild dance. All the girls started dancing and everything was back to normal.

That's why I loved my neighborhood, we were all family. I peeped Chelle observing me, I acted like I didn't see her. She didn't know I knew she was watching me.

I just stood there as she started approaching where I was. My hip vibrated, it was my beeper. I looked down at the number, at first, I thought it was Sandman, but it wasn't. I didn't recognize the number.

"Anybody got a cell phone on them?" I yelled out.

Nobody answered, as I hopped off the wall and headed to my car. I heard a soft voice, "You can use my house phone."

I turned with my keys in hand and saw Chelle.

"Damn she live up here." I spoke quietly. I ain't never seen her ass.

As if she was reading my mind, she said. "I just move up here with my sister Tay."

"Nah I got to make a run anyway, but thanks." I said. Before I got in my car, I turned back and asked her. "Do I know you from somewhere?" Before, she could answer, I shook my head. "Nah!" Got in my car and pulled off. I could see the look in her eyes, I had her curious now.

I drove down the street and parked around the back of my building. I got out and walked to my apartment. As I entered I peeked in.

Big Doris's room door was closed, she must have been asleep. I walked in the living room and grabbed the phone. I started dialing the number 3-0-1-8-5-3-0-9-7-3. I heard a ring, then two.

"Hello." A deep male voice answered.

"Yeah somebody paged me?" I asked.

"Nah! Who is me?" asked the male voice.

I was skeptical about giving my name. So, I politely said. "Sorry wrong number."

"A'ight man." The male voice said then hung up.

I sat contemplating on what was up wit' that shit. I locked the number in my pager for some reason, that right there tingled my senses.

CHAPTER EIGHTEEN

Friday 12:30 p.m.

The sun was beaming, I was outside standing on the maze watching pipe head Peanut wash my Z. A youngin' named Duck from 57th Place southeast had sold me four brand spanking new thirteen inch chrome deep dish classic rims for my Z.

They fit perfectly, I went to the body shop off of U street southeast and had my windows tinted. I had a Kentwood Radio installed with four tweeters and one big six by nine speaker in the back. My joint was customized just like I'd imagined. My passenger door was opened, Peanut was washing the rims.

Franky Beverly and Maze jammed from the speakers. Peanut was in the zone washing and dancing. Peanut was chubby and black as tar. He was the hood car cleaner. I stood on the wall fly as shit. Junkyard was playing tonight at the Ibex.

Everybody was getting prepared. I had on a pair of green and white Eddie Bauer cargo shorts, with a linked all chrome heavy belt. A fresh pair of slouch socks with a fresh pair of white Air Force Ones, with green outlining to match my shorts.

I had on a white Abercrombie and Fitch T-shirt, with colorful designs in the middle and a Philadelphia Eagles fitted cap, and a 10k all chrome watch matching my belt. Today I was dressed to impress. I stood on the wall thinking about what I was going to do for today. I had some yay, so I might as well get some money, until tonight.

"Here ya keys youngsta." Peanut said breaking my train of thought.

I looked at my car, it was gleaming. I saw the pride in Peanut's eyes, I liked what I saw. I pulled out my knot of money and gave Peanut a hundred-dollar bill.

"Ohh…thank you shorty." Peanut said smiling. "I needed this to buy me some food and clothes for me and my ole lady." Peanut said.

I always looked out for the pipe heads. I guess that's why I had so many customers. I'll give them money sometimes to feed their kids. Some spent it genuinely and some went and bought more crack. I learned the hard way about giving money, but if they earned it I had no problem wit' it. Peanut stepped off whistling the Franky Beverly and Maze tune. I hopped off the wall and walked to my car.

"Wooo… this baby clean." I whistled.

I opened the door and got in, I inhaled the fresh scent of incense and some concoction of shit Peanut put together. I started the car up and drove off.

As I was driving to get something to eat. I decided to go down to Division Ave to the carry out. Everybody was on the Ave deep, niggas were hustling, or just standing around. I parked in front of the carry out and walked in.

"What's up Lil' Fox." A voice called out.

I looked, and it was Mike, that nigga that was up Ridge Road that night in the hallway. He had on a black Skully, black gloves, blue jeans, and black Timberland boots. He was leaning to the far side of the wall in the carryout.

"What's happening, Joe?" I responded.

This time I had my .40 caliber on my hip.

"That you right there?" He asked pointing to my ZX.

"Yeah that's me." I replied.

"That joint look sweet." Mike said.

"Yeahhh…" I bragged.

"Yeah that joint proper!" He said.

"Thanks Joe." I stepped to the glass to order my food. "Can I get a double cheese burger with everything on it and a strawberry-Kiwi Mistic?" I asked, then paid the cashier.

I could see Mike behind me in the reflection of the glass, staring at my car. I turned around Mike looked at me, he didn't say a word, but I felt his envy. I looked out the window till the cashier brought my order. I thanked him, said goodbye to Mike and left.

As I was walking to my car, I noticed a pretty female with some grocery bags and a child in her arm, coming out of the grocery store next door.

I kept stepping, started my car, and was waiting for the traffic to clear a lane when a knock came at my passenger window. I always kept my gun in my lap. I thought it was Mike, but it was the pretty girl. That pretty girl was Chelle, I rolled my window down to see what the fuck she wanted.

"Yeah, what's up Joe?" I asked.

"Fox can you please help me?" Chelle asked.

"Help you…help you with what?" I asked. "If you need some money to catch the bus here you." I reached in my ashtray and handed her a hand full of change.

After I handed her the change, before she had a chance to respond I saw a lane had cleared and I peeled off.

I looked in my rearview mirror and saw her jumping up and down.

"No, I need a ride for me and my daughter." She screamed.

"Fuck that bitch." I grumbled and kept driving, but her voice was in my head.

"Me and my daughter!" Her voice echoed.

"Shit!" I cursed aloud.

I bucked a U at the light and drove back to get her.

When I went back in front of the carryout she was gone. As I turned around the corner there she was sitting at the bus stop, with the little infant in her arms.

I drove up and stopped in front of her. She looked ready to attack me. She also looked sexy when she pouted. I was hoping she said something, but she looked at me and turned her head. I opened the passenger side door to her. She didn't move I was getting irritated now. I don't know what made me do it, but I turned on my hazard lights and got out.

"Girl get yo' ass in the car." I said as I grabbed her grocery bags. You ain't gonna have me waiting for your ass."

She didn't protest or hesitate, she got up and sat in the passenger seat with the baby quietly. When I finished putting the last bag in, I got in the car and pulled off. She didn't say anything at first and I didn't offer any conversation. As we were driving, she finally opened her mouth.

"That's fucked up how you tried to carry me with my daughter Young." She said.

"Well, I remember a few weeks ago you and your little girlfriends tried to carry me." I reminded her.

"Oh yeah." She said with a stupid look on her face.

"Remember that?" I asked. "Don't ever judge a book by its cover. Now we're even." I said.

Chelle didn't say nothing 'cause I was right. She felt stupid.

"Girl I didn't know you had a baby." I told her.

Chelle looked towards the window. "Yeah, my baby's father bitch ass just got locked up around 21st."

"Sorry to hear that. What's her name?" I asked.
"Karima."

"What the fuck kinda name is that?" I asked myself silently.

As if she could sense my question, she replied. "Her father's name is Kareem."

"Oh okay. I was just thinking about her name." I admitted.

She directed me to the front of her building.

I got out, grabbed her grocery bags, and helped her into the apartment. They lived on the first floor to the left. As soon as I walked in about three kids flew past me.

"What the fuck was that?" I said. "I know them wasn't kids moving that fast." My mind was roaming, they scared the shit out of me.

They were hiding behind the couch, peaking at me. The apartment wasn't neat, shit was everywhere, clothes, shoes, paper, and more.

"You'll have to excuse the place right now." Chelle said.

I took the groceries into the kitchen while Chelle put her daughter in her crib.

"If you want you can eat in the kitchen." Chelle yelled from the back room.

The kitchen was at least clean. She came walking in, she had taken her shoes off, her sexy feet were showing. I looked down and felt myself getting aroused.

"Here take a seat." Chelle offered, pushing a chair my way.

"Nah, I'm a'ight...I gotta roll, I'll eat in my car." I told her as I started to leave.

Chelle followed me to the door. "Boy you sure?" She asked in a sincere voice. "Why you leaving? You can take some time to eat." She looked directly into my eyes.

I turned away from her penetrating stare. "I appreciate it, but I'm already running jive late. Thanks anyway!" I said and left.

Chelle stood in the doorway and watched me leave. As I got in my car, I could still see Chelle staring at me. I started the engine and drove off, this was too close for comfort.

I was in front of my building hustling when Snuk pulled up in a '92' Acura white on white Coup. It had mirror tints and a set of hammer rims.

"Ooooh...that joint sweet." I said as he parked behind my Nissan 300ZX turbo.

Snuk was now slinging yay out in Maryland. I hadn't seen him in a little while now.

"Damn bro, when did you cop the coupe?" I asked.

"I had this joint for 'bout two and half weeks now." Snuk said.

"This joint reminds me of Bama old Ac." I said.

"I see you not doing too bad yo' self." Snuk said. "That yo' Z right there?" He pointed.

"Yeah Joe, ery' body sweating that joint." I boasted proudly. "How's the princess?" I asked.

"Baby girl a mess...she tryna walk and everything." Snuk replied proudly.

"Yeah I gotta stop by your spot to pay some respect to my niece." I said. "I've been...hold up bro." I said as a pipe head walked up. "What's up?" I asked.

"Uh...I got seventy-five bones...can ya do some 'em wit' em?" The skinny crackhead asked.

"Of course." I said as I put my hand out for the money.

Once I had the money in my possession, I counted it. It was seventy-five dollars exactly. I reached behind the wall to my hidden stash spot, then handed him five jumbo sized pieces of crack. His eyes watered wit' anticipation as he saw the size of the rocks.

"T...t...thank you youngin'." He said as he hurried off.

"Yeah now back to what I was saying bro...I been procrastinating on getting to ya crib." I told Snuk as we resumed our conversation. "Yeah you know I'ma stop through tho."

"Yeah, I know," Snuk said.

As we were kicking it, Mickey came strutting up. Boy was I glad to see him because I wanted my paper and his ass had been M.I.A.

"What's up Shawdy?" Mickey spoke as he tried to walk by me as if it was just a regular day.

"Hold...hold...up Mickey!" I said, stepping in front of him, blocking his path. "Nigga where's my money." I asked.

"Whatcha a fuckin' pimp now?" He retorted sarcastically.

"Nigga you better watch ya muthafuckin mouth." Snuk said angrily. "Now answer my lil' brother."

"Snuk like I explained, I'm waiting on my income tax check." I got him." Mickey said nervously.

"You betta get me or I'ma get you." I warned Mickey as we walked up the building stairs. "I'ma fuck that nigga up." I told Snuk.

"Yeah and I'ma help you." Snuk agreed.

CHAPTER NINETEEN

'Women you can't live with 'em...can't live without 'em'!

Another week flew past, I was on the block hustling when my pager went off. *'Man who could this be'?* I was thinking. I grabbed my beeper and looked at the number.

I didn't recognize it, so I was curious. I hopped in my car and drove to Benning Road Subway Station phone booth. I get to the phone booth and dialed the number. A female voice picked up and answered.

"Man, who dis?" I asked.

"This Keisha."

"Where the fuck you been!" I yelled.

"Fox, I told you I had to take care of my grandmother." Keisha replied.

"Why the fuck you playing on a nigga conscious like I'm green or something Keisha!" I snapped.

"Look Fox we need to talk. I'm sorry I haven't called you." She said.

"So, what am I supposed to be second to your games?" I asked, the pain trembled in my voice. "I ain't no half ass nigga, Keisha. You can deal with them other niggas like that, but not me. So just continue to do what makes you happy." I told her.

"Nigga you make me happy." Keisha screamed crying.

"Keisha this stunt you pulled ain't fair." I continued.

"Fox, you I love you, you know how I feel about you." Keisha whined.

"No, I don't, I've been worried about you, thinking about you. I don't see my girl anymore. Fuck, I shouldn't have fell in love wit' your ass." I fussed.

"Nigga you don't mean that after what we shared." Keisha whined.

"Well, you might be right, but it sounds good right about now."

"Oh, I hate your ass because I love you so much!"

"Maann... tell that shit to the next nigga." I snapped. Keisha where the fuck you been for two months." I asked.

"Boy I just had to get away to find myself and what I really wanted." She replied.

"What's the fuck, you think this shit is...days of our lives or something! What about me, your nigga, my muthafuckin' feelings. Huh that's some selfish shit." I told her.

I was really started to lose my cool. I would've been hung up the phone, but the curiosity of where she was captured my attention.

"Fox do you love me?" Keisha asked.

"What the fuck kinda question is that? Keisha girl you know good damn well I love your selfish ass. Now, answer my fuckin' question...where have you been?" I asked again.

Keisha began mumbling and crying.

"Keisha you gonna make me call you a bitch, now answer me!" I yelled. She kept crying. "Maann...fuck this shit! You ain't gonna string me like a puppet. Youngin' be easy!" I hung up the phone.

Before I hung up I heard Keisha mumble. "I love you!"

"Fuck that shit." I grumbled. If she didn't want to speak to me she could speak to the dial tone. "I'm out!"

****

A nigga gotta get that money, I wasn't taking no muthafuckin' shorts. I'm back at it on my grind, hustlin'. I used this to block Keisha out of my head. I was free to do what I wanted now.

"Hey youngsta, you workin' wit's some 'em?" a pipe head asked me.

"Yeah, lova whatcha need?" I responded.

"Let me get two for fifteen." He said.

"Nah lova you can take that two for fifteen shit up tha street." I told him. "I got boulders for shoulders on this end."

"Le' me see." Asked the pipe head.

"What the fuck is you heated or some 'em?" I asked angrily. "Nigga assume the position now!" I yelled, pulling out my gun.

"N...n...nah, youngin' it ain't nothing like that." He stuttered scared, assuming the position anyway.

I thoroughly pat searched him. He came up clean, I'd never seen this pipe head before so I had to shake him down. Sandman been put me on point about undercovers posing as crackheads.

"Youngin' I'm just trying to blow my lungs."

"Alright give me that money." I said.

He handed me the fifteen dollars and I broke him off something proper. "Now beat ya feet lova."

"T...t...thank you." He was still stuttering scared, as he hurriedly dashed away.

Keisha kept blowing my box up, paging me. I tried my best to ignore her pages. I was on some Michael Jackson shit. She's out of my life was the song in my head. Bitches was scandalous, I'ma keeping it moving, for today.

I was down on Division Ave selling dope for Sandman.

"Holla if ya hear me. I got dat work! I got dat work!" I yelled.

As I was about to 'round the corner, a black BMW 535i pulled up to the curve.

"Hey youngsta, you on call?" A pretty white lady that looked to be in her mid-twenties asked.

"Holla if ya hear me." I responded.

That was my code for yes, on the Ave. saying yes was never to be used for security purposes. She looked at me smiling, she had a perfect straight line of teeth. I really couldn't believe, she wanted to buy some dope. She asked for five twenty bags. I was hesitant to serve her, but dope fiends came in all colors, shapes, and sizes.

"Go 'round the corner but get outta ya car and walk." I instructed her.

"Okay." She happily responded.

As I walked around the corner, I saw the white girl coming towards my way. At first, I was going to rob her, but I decided not to.

I went to my stash, when I came back she was there waiting on me biting her nails. I turned over my hand for the money. She gave it to me, I then gave her the bags of dope. She thanked me but stood right there. I was then getting nervous.

"Wh…what's up girlfriend?" I asked.

"Aren't you too young to be selling dope?" She asked.

"Ain't you too young to be doin' dope?" I responded. Hold…bitch fuck is you five-o?" I pulled out my Glock.

At sight of the gun she jumped back, but then she shocked me when she ripped her shit open, poppin' the buttons on her expensive shirt and all. "No!" She said in a stern voice. "I don't play that police shit."

"Then don't ask me 'bout my muthafuckin' business." I warned and kept looking at her breasts in her sexy black bra. "Cover yourself up." I told her. She did as I told her. "What's your name?" I asked her.

"Megan." She replied.

"Look Megan, I'm at work so can you excuse me." I asked. She kept looking at me. "What do you want bitch!" I asked getting irritated.

"I want to only buy from you." She said. "You seem real, I like that."

After hearing that I was all for it. My whole demeanor changed.

"My bad for snapping at you, it's just I been tried." I told her.

"I understand, give me your number, so I can contact you." She replied.

"Nah." I declined. "Give me your number so I can contact you." I told her.

She reached in her purse and got a pen and napkin to write her number down.

"Aww... fuck it take this pager number." I said. "I'll get your number when you hit me on the hip."

She smiled that perfect smile as I gave her the number.

"I'll call you." Megan said.

"Alright." I gave her my old pager number. That pager just sits in my house.

As she walked away, I felt relaxed. I didn't have a bad feeling about her. I was hyped up for the day, I'd met a new connect maybe.

It was nearing shut down time. I was standing in front of Barnett's when three beautiful young females came my way. I knew one of them. The one I knew name was Tesha nicknamed Watergate, for what reason I don't know. She was from the 58th projects, several blocks down from my hood Lincoln Heights. She went to H.D. Woodson Senior High school. The other two girls were her cousins that came to visit her from Southwest.

"Heey... Fox!" Watergate spoke.

Now Watergate wasn't no ten piece, but she was definitely on eight wit' potential. She was 5'4, brown-skinned, with almond eyes, and short hair. Her style of dress wasn't that fly, but her titties, and phat ass made up for that. She had this little cute nose that made her look like a little munchkin or a squirrel. She was definitely cute, so I decided to play her game.

"What's up girlfriend?" I responded.

"Nothing, what you doing down here boy?" Watergate asked.

"Minding my business. What y'all girls up to?" I asked.

"We just getting some 'em to eat." Watergate's cousin responded, with a hint of lust in her eyes.

Her name was Tish from 3rd Street southeast. She was dark-skinned, about 5'5, weave in her hair, dressed in a short jean skirt, exposing some thick thighs, with a pink halter top.

Her girl Reebok Classics was sparkling white. Tish was chewing some bubble gum looking at me seductively behind Watergate's back.

I made a mental note, that I had to sex this pretty young thing. Watergate's other cousin didn't bother to give me her name and pretended to be bored., I ignored her skinny red ass. I'd been making political moves all day, so my pockets had the mumps.

"Let me pay for y'all food." I told them.

They all obliged, Watergate instructed her cousins to go pay for the food while she stayed outside with me and talked. I gave her cousin Tish a fifty-dollar bill and told her to keep the change.

She bit her bottom lip and looked up at me with those slanted flirty eyes. I turned my gaze to Watergate because I wanted to get in her panties first. I'd holla at Tish another time.

"So, what's up witcha?" I asked Watergate.

"You." She responded.

"Oh yeah," I smiled. "Girl you so cute." Watergate blushed at my compliment.

"Well I heard your girl cute too." She replied.

"What!" I responded. "Maan… I'm like Patti Labelle, on my own. I'm free to do as I please."

"Oh yeah, le' me find out then. So, what happened wit' y'all Fox?"

"Man, it's a long story and too short of a time to tell it." I answered.

"Well I'm coming up the Heights this weekend, maybe you can tell it to me then."

"Maybe I can, here's my beeper number. Hit me on my hip." I told her.

She smiled as I started walking away.

"Bye Fox."

I looked, and her cousin Tish coming out of the carryout.

"See ya shawty." I responded.

Watergate had started coming around Lincoln Heights to see me. She was cool, and we kept it like that.

"Damn young you let that dirty ass bitch come 'round dis joint hollering your name and shit." Tye said.

We were sitting in front of my building on the maze's wall. Just me and some fellas were out there hustlin' that night.

"Joe shorty cool." I responded.

"Fuck dat, that bitch look like an embarrassment. Plus, I heard she was fucking with B.J." Tye said.

"Man chill da fuck out, she ain't bun-bun nigga. I'm free as a bird." I told Tye.

"Well don't get ya feathers plucked fuckin' wit' this one." Tye spat.

"Nigga pump ya brakes. I'm straight." I assured Tye.

This nigga Tye didn't like Watergate for some reason and she felt the same way about him.

I was waiting on Watergate to pull up. She said, she was going to come chill wit' a nigga. As me and the fellas was talking my pager beeped. I looked at the number and it was Keisha again. I immediately erased it.

"Fuck dis bitch keep hitting me for?" I spoke aloud.

"What?" The fellas asked in unison.

"Nothin' y'all I'm just speaking aloud." I said.

We continued to chill when a grey van pulled up and parked at the curve. Watergate and some of her 58th homegirls hopped out the van. Niggas heads lifted and everybody went to smiling. Those niggas were happy.

"It's about to be a party. Nigga go get some drink and blunts." My man Greg hollered.

All the guys and girls matched up as Watergate walked straight up to me and hugged me. She smelled so good.

"Hey sweetheart." I said.

"Hey Fox." She responded.

"I thought you wasn't coming." I told her.

"Boy, I had to pick up these bitches." She said.

I laughed, me and Watergate talked for a while. She just kept her arms around my waist and her head in my chest, while we talked. She looked so cute in her fitted sweatshirt.

I had one some Polo sweatpants and a Polo long-sleeve T-shirt, with some all-white low cut Air Force Ones. Watergate's body heat felt good against mine. She looked up with those sexy puppy eyes and I kissed her cute little nose.

Watergate smiled, "Let's go in your house." She whispered.

"Hold up." Big Doris in there." I told her.

"Who is Big Doris?" Watergate asked.

"That's my mama."

Watergate busted out laughing.

"Naw girl you betta take Big Doris serious." I warned.

Watergate kept laughing.

"A'ight come on." I pulled her hand as we crept into my building, ducking her friends who were too busy having a good time to notice our disappearance.

As I put the key in the lock and opened the door. I shushed Watergate with one finger to my lips.

She silently nodded. I crept in the back to Big Doris's room. She was out cold, snoring like a mad Bull. I eased Big Doris door close. I motioned Watergate to go into my room, to the right.

She followed my motion. Once I got to my room and closed the door, Me and Watergate both giggled like little kids. My room was dark and I didn't want to cut that bright ass light on. It would have alerted our friends outside of my window. I decided to keep it off.

Watergate's eyes adjusted to the dark and she sat down on my bed. I sat beside her, Watergate pulled me on top of her and we started kissing. We kissed passionately, then I felt Watergate grab my dick and squeeze it. I was rock hard, Watergate pulled her skirt off as I pulled my sweatpants down.

I reached around in the dark on my dresser for a condom. I found one, popped it, and slid it down my dick. I laid back over Watergate as she grabbed my dick and put it in the entrance of her vagina. I pushed in her slowly as she spread her legs wider.

"Oooh...Fox!" She gasped.

I pushed further, her hands grabbed the back of my shoulders tight. I began to pump hard, back and forth, back and forth.

"Oooh...Fox...oooo...Fox! Baby...ooohhh...baby!" Watergate kept moaning.

"Girl your ass betta be quiet fo' you get me and yo' ass beat by Big Doris." I whispered.

"Damn boy this shit feels so good!" She whispered.

I kissed her and continued to pump. I felt a nut coming on, so I pushed Watergate's legs up and started punishing that pussy. She was biting her lip to muffle her moans of ecstasy. I bent down and buried my face in her neck to muffle my groan as I came. Watergate stroked my back soothingly.

"Damn!" I mumbled.

We just laid there for a minute, until I remembered Big Doris.

"Come on girl." I whispered.

My whole pubic area was wet. Damn she came hard as shit. As I pulled her into my bathroom. It wasn't cum I saw, it was blood. She was on her period, when she saw the blood on me. she looked so embarrassed. I wanted to yell but I didn't. I just squeezed her hand and told her don't worry, I understood it was a woman's thing.

She kept trying to apologize. "I...I...I'm so sorry Fox. I meant it. I'm so sorry." She started crying.

I hugged her. "Like I said I understand. It's a part of nature. They way God cleanse women." I told her and handed her a towel with a bar of ivory soap as me and her quietly washed up.

I went back to my room cut on my bright ass light and found both of us some clean sweat pants to wear. Watergate folded her underwear and skirt and took them with her. I made sure my room and bathroom were clean before I followed her back outside. Her friends were outside my building waiting with a million and one questions.

I kissed Watergate on her forehead, she smiled as her and friends walked to the van to leave.

"I'ma call you later Fox!" She called out.

"A'ight!" I said as I turned to go back upstairs.

"Nigga you hit that?" Tye asked in disbelief.

All the fellas were ear hustlin' hard as a muthafucka. A dead silence filled the air until I spoke up.

"Hell yeah!" I hollered.

Everybody broke out with daps and high fives. Tye just shook his head.

"And the pussy was the bomb!" I yelled before leaving.

That was no lie, Watergate had some good pussy.

CHAPTER TWENTY

I was doing good as a muthafucka and no matter how you try to hide it, it tends to come unconsciously. I went down to 46th Street Northeast to holla at my mans and 'em. Saadiq and Light-skinned Mike. My man pretty boy Rome was out there too, chilling.

It was blazing outside so niggas was using less energy as possible.

I pulled up and parked my car, "What's up y'all?" I asked as I walked to the end of the alley where everybody was chilling.

"Shit!"

"Nothing!"

"Just laying."

Were their responses. Rome was laying on top of an '87' Box Nissan Maxima. Rashad and Saadiq were standing up clockin' sales.

"Fox the Heights bringing you that money huh?" Saadiq asked.

"I'm doing a little some' em…some 'em!" I boasted.

"Man, the Heights be going hard, them niggas up there be trippin'." Rashad said.

"Man, you know how that shit is." I replied. "Niggas gonna be niggas just like animals gonna be animals. Ya feel me?"

Everybody nodded in agreement.

"Fox what's up wit' cha girl, shorty wit' those pretty green eyes?" Rome asked.

"Man, I kicked that bitch to the curb." I shot back.

"Stop playin' Fox, not the bun-bun!" Rome said.

"Nah, Young this bitch went AWOL for two months and didn't even call a nigga. Who da fuck she think she playin' wit?" I said.

"What did she say about her whereabouts?" Rashad asked.

"She told me she was over her fuckin' grandmother's house finding herself or some shit like that. I told that bitch for all I care she could stay lost."

"Oooo…" Saadiq said. "Damn Fox you cold hearted"

"Joe, you shoulda at least let her explain herself." Rashad suggested.

"About what, man no bitch playin' me like a chump. That's that sucka shit. Ya feel me?"

Everybody again nodded in agreement. As we were talking a dude stepped out of the doorway of one of the houses along the alley.

He was brown-skinned and had on a pair of blue jeans and a designer white t-shirt. He walked toward the car that Rome was laying on top of. Rome had his hands behind his head, just laying there chilling, rapping wit' us.

"Excuse me main man." The dude asked Rome.

"Oh, my fault cuz." Rome said and started to get up.

Another dude came out the doorway. He was telling a broad, he'd catch up with her later. He had on a pair of black jeans and a black T-shirt with gold trimming, and some Timbs. As he exited the door he saw Rome getting ready to get off the car hood.

"Hey man get the fuck off my car, slim!" He yelled.

The dude's partner tried to tell him that Rome was just about to get off the car.

"Man lay back." His partner tried to calm him down.

"Joe, who the fuck you talking too?" Rome shot back at him.

"You nigga! I don't see no owls out this bitch in the day time lova." He barked.

"You betta pipe yo' ass down, nigga." Rome warned.

"Nigga fuck you and get the fuck off my shit!" the dude continued.

Rome looked over at us, "Do this nigga live round here?" he asked.

"Naw."

"Not that I know of."

"Neva seen the bama."

"Can't live in this area!"

We all responded.

"Nigga where the fuck you from Maryland?" Rome asked. "Cause ain't no Maryland nigga runnin' shit on this end. Ya man was real polite in his approach and I respect him for that, but cuz you definitely barking up the wrong tree."

"Bitch ass nigga, just slide off my shit." The dude responded.

"Come on Rome, let it go young." I told Rome.

Rome reluctantly got off the hood of the car and walked over by us. The dude and his partner proceeded to walk to the car, still mumbling. I was just hoping that the dudes left before it got hectic.

As the dude was getting in his driver side door, it looked like he reached and pulled an object out of his waist.

"Oh, bitch ass nigga, you got a joint...you got a joint!" Rome fumed. "Anybody out here got their hamma?" Rome asked.

I kept heat on like a stove. "Yeah young." I said as I handed Rome a .380 caliber gun.

Rome quickly took the gun, switched the safety off, and pulled the trigger. *Pop...Pop...Pop...Pop...* the gun roared.

The dudes ducked down in the car as windows exploded. Rome handed me back the gun as me, him, Rashad, and Saadiq ran up the alley. As we were running up the alley Rome was talkin' shit.

"That'll teach them bitch ass niggas!" We heard gravel rattling and the sound of a car coming behind us fast.

"Go...go...go...go...go!" I yelled.

It was the dudes, all the shots Rome fired missed them and just hit the car. From then on everything happened in slow motion. The car came speeding up fast. Rome hopped a fence to the right and ran through some neighbor's yard. He got away but the car kept coming after us.

We were just trying to make it to Rashad and Saadiq's grandmother's house. It was the next house, Saadiq and Rashad had made it. I was the last, as I was running I knew I had only six shots left.

I hopped the fence to Rashad and Saadiq's back yard and my sweatpants pocket got caught in the fence, which propelled me forward. As I was in motion falling the white 87 Nissan Maxima pulled up with the dudes.

Damn sure enough he had a gun in his hand. It was a silver and black .38 revolver. He had a grimace on his face, I knew I was dead. I closed my eyes, while in midair. I was damn near upside down, and I fired my gun.

Pop...Pop...Pop...Pop...!

I landed on the back of my neck, my pants ripped on the gate, which caused me to do a front flip. For a good two seconds, I laid there waiting for death to fall upon me.

Once I realized there wasn't no return fire, I scrambled up and hauled ass to Rashad and Saadiq's back door. We all made it in safely, my neck was bruised, but I wasn't trippin', as long as I was alive.

"Damn Young, you smashed cuz." Saadiq said.

I looked out the back window and was shocked when I saw the dude's head resting on the steering wheel, with blood oozing out of it from the bullet wounds. His hand was hanging outside the window with the pistol still in it.

"Damn Joe." I whispered. My heart was beating so fast. "What happened to his partner?" I asked.

"When you was rocking off, slim jumped out the passenger door and jetted." Rashad said.

"Man, you gots ta bounce. Five-O will be here in a minute." Saadiq said.

"Young take my dirt bike and leave your car down here. Hurry up nigga!" Rashad yelled.

I went to the shed out back, grabbed Rashad's pink and white Honda CR 80 Motorbike and ran it out of the alley until I got to the end. Then I started it, put it in first gear, and balled out. I pushed it to the limit, that bad boy was fast too.

As I was riding home, I thought damn why everything I do good is always all bad.

I told Snuk about what had just happened with the murder. I thought he was going to go off, but to my surprise he remained calm.

"Shorty you got to do what you got to do, sometimes. Niggas ain't sympathizing in these streets. It's either kill or be killed. You handled your business." Snuk replied. "Give me your car keys, I'll go pick your car up for you."

I threw Snuk my car keys, Snuk left, I kept Rashad's bike. I'd return it later.

Niggas was bored to death on the block. Everybody wanted money, but everybody couldn't get money. I had returned Rashad's bike and the murder went unsolved. It felt like a burden was lifted off of my shoulders.

"Man a Go-Go band playing up 57th recreation center tonight." Greg told us.

"Oh yeah." Tye said.

"Yeah, young so you know there's gonna be some bitches up dat joint. What y'all tryna do?" Greg asked.

"Man, we tryna party." Omar said.

"Young I'm in." I said.

"I'll go and see what they hitting on." Black Mike said.

"Let's do da muthafucka." Pee-Wee chipped in.

Everybody else agreed, so we were on our way to 57th rec Go-Go.

"Let's go get ready y'all." Tye said.

CHAPTER TWENTY-ONE

We pulled up and packed down the street from the rec, so that just in case something jumped off we could have space to get ghost. Me and the fellas walked through the entrance to the sound of the bass drum kicking, to congas rocking.

"Where y'all from…what…where y'all from!" Was being shouted from the huge speakers as the head maestro was chanting to the beat.

People from all over that area was yelling where they was from.

"Clay Terrance! U-58th, 46th Place, Division Ave, East Gate, 57th, Simple City, Benning Road, Call Place!"

We came in the door deep.

"There go those Lincoln Heights boys." One girl whispered.

As the roll call was getting funky, my man Tye hollered out. "All Lincoln Heights…all Lincoln Heights!"

Everybody that came with us joined in, "All Lincoln Heights! All Lincoln Heights!" We yelled.

The lead maestro yelled, "Who dat dere! I say who dat dere! Is that Lincoln Heights! That's what I like!" The band began, but I wasn't feeling the atmosphere.

Too many niggas were eye fucking us more than the bitches. I kept a pocket knife, but I wasn't there for no drama. I just wanted to have a good time. I started to feel uncomfortable. I told the fellas I was gonna head out.

Tye pulled me aside, he had been sweating from dancing. "Squirrel, you a'ight Joe?"

"Yeah, Young I'm straight, I'm just 'bout to bounce. Y'all niggas stay and party. I got my hamma in the car and I got my knife in my pocket." I said.

"A'ight Joe, I'ma catch up wit' cha later." Tye said.

As we were about to walk off I heard someone calling out my name. "Fox is that you?" a female's voice called out from the crowd.

The voice walked forward, it was Watergate.

"Damn what the fuck, is you this nigga fairy God mother or some 'em?" Tye yelled to be heard over the loud speakers.

"Fuck you Tye." Watergate shot.

"Yeah...yeah...yeah, I heard it all before, but your shit ain't working now."

"Nigga w...whatever please!" Watergate said as she threw up her hand in Tye's face to block him out.

"Bitch!" Tye yelled. "You betta get ya hand outta my face before I break it."

"What you think I'm scared of you Tye?" Watergate wasn't backing down.

"Hold...hold...hold..." I stepped in the middle of Watergate and Tye.

"Squirrel you betta check that bitch like a beeper." I couldn't help but laugh at Tye's crazy ass.

"I got her young, gone and get ya party on. I'll catch ya later." I said. I gave Tye some dap and a hug and stepped off, Watergate. "Calm down baby girl, your lil' ass is feisty." I told her.

"Nah, ya man always got some' em to say to me." Watergate said.

"Just stay away from him before y'all get into it." I suggested after I released her shoulders.

"Nigga what, I'm ready." She said standing there looking all cute. "I'll see anybody."

"Well let me hip you to Tye, that nigga ain't anybody. He gonna fight you just as hard as he'll fight a nigga. That nigga doesn't give a fuck if you're a girl or not. Believe me he don't see that shit. That nigga crazy." I warned laughing.

"Well he can bring it." Watergate said defiantly.

I laughed again. "Girl you are wild. Dig I'ma about to roll so stay away from Tye and stay your butt outta trouble." I told her.

"Where you going boo, I haven't seen you in a minute, plus I haven't even talked to you come to think of it." She pleaded.

"I'm out this joint, my head rocking." I lied.

"Excuse me slim." A skinny young grimy looking dude squeezed past us. I peeped how he looked at Watergate then me. I saw the look many of times.

I'ma new nigga around their hood talking to their hood rat. This is bound to be trouble, I really had to go now.

"Look I'll call you later." I told her as I started to walk off.

"Nah, your head hurt you're coming over my house. I live right up the street from here." She grabbed my hand and headed for the exit before I got a chance to protest.

We exited the building and I headed towards my car.

"Boy where you going?" she asked.

"Nah my car down the street we can drive to your spot." I told her.

"Oh okay." She agreed.

As we headed down the street I looked back at the rec entrance door and saw the young grimy dude burst out the door with a pack of other youngins, looking in both directions. We were a ways down the street near my car. They couldn't see us, I was glad, I got in my car and unlocked the passenger side door for Watergate. I grabbed my Glock .40 from under my seat.

"Damn boy, what you need that for?" She questioned.

"Never know sweetheart, you never know." I started the ignition and pulled out of the parking space.

We drove up and stopped at the light. The light was across the street from the recreation center. I could still see the dudes curious looks. They were looking everywhere wondering where had me and Watergate disappeared to. On the inside of me I was laughing.

"Your head still hurting boo?" Watergate asked breaking my trance. She started massaging my neck with one hand.

"A little but I'm a'ight."

The light turned green and we drove pass the idiots to her house.

We arrived at Watergate's house, I parked, got out, and walk with her to her front door. She opened the door and we entered. The house was spacious and cozy. She had two lamps, that gave the living room a relaxing vibe.

"Anybody home?" Watergate called out.

"Only me." A lady responded from upstairs.

"Oh, Fox that's my aunt, she came to visit from Southwest."

Her aunt came downstairs and to my amazement she was fine as wine.

"Girl what stray you bringing home now?" The lady asked Watergate.

"Oh, aunt Rita this is my friend Fox. He from Lincoln Heights."

"How are you doing Aunt Rita?" I asked smiling.

She started blushing, "Boy, I ain't old, I'm twenty-three, so call me Rita."

"Oh, my bad." I said.

"I brought him up here because his head is hurting." Watergate said. "We just came from the Go-Go at 57th Rec."

"Girl I'm headed that way now." Her aunt Rita informed. "Boy I got some 'em for that headache. You smoke weed?"

"Off and on." I told her.

"Well smoke dis, dis shit will have that headache gone and you high as a kite." She reached in her purse and pulled out a big ass Ziploc bag of weed, sacked up in five-dollar bag.

She popped the Ziploc bag open, reached inside, and handed me three five-dollar sacks.

I smelled it. "Hmmm…smells crucial." I complimented.

"Yeah that's that Oooh-La-La from southwest." She bragged.

"Preciate it!" I told her.

"Watergate girl I'm 'bout to go down there and get my party on. I'll see y'all later." Rita said as she exited out the front door.

"Come on boy." Watergate ordered, grabbing my hand, leading me upstairs to her bedroom.

Her room was small, but cozy, it was girlish, with teddy bears on a dresser, a big mirror on another dresser, pink, white, blue, and odd brown colors surrounded the room.

I walked to one wall which was covered with photos of people in the Go-Go and dudes I knew. Some were dead, a lot of the dudes was in prison. Here was a lot of pictures and memories.

"Boy, let's roll that shit up." Watergate suggested.

I handed her the bags of weed, she rolled like a magician. We smoked the weed and I laid back on her bed, with my hands behind head.

"Boo, your headache gone?" She asked.

"A little bit." I said groggily. I was high as a kite.

Watergate crawled on top of me. "So, you gonna be my bun-bun or what?" She asked kissing my neck.

"I'm still thinking 'bout dat right dere!" I said.

"Come on Fox, you know I like you," she said. "I know you like me too, stop faking nigga."

"It ain't that Watergate, I...I like you, but you fuckin' wit' B.J. you know that's my homey from the hood." I told her.

"What...I don't fuck no B.J. That nigga old news Fox. I swear on everything." She lifted my shirt and was now licking my navel coming up the middle of my stomach to my chest.

"Take your clothes off." She whispered.

I slowly complied, my mind was in a haze. Next thing I knew we were butt naked. Watergate was riding me hard, I grabbed her small waist and pushed deeper into her pussy. She pulled me up to her as I wrapped my arms around her waist and passionately kissed me. She was moaning loud.

"Get in doggy style." I told her.

I pulled her hair as I fucked her from behind. We had a lot of time to try all positions. After several nuts later, we just laid there in bed exhausted. Watergate laid in my arms with one leg in between mine.

"Damn boy, you can fuck." She whispered.

I was still high as a kite, I didn't even respond. She kissed my chest as I fell asleep.

****

The next morning, I woke up to the smell of fried eggs and bacon.

"Damn I can't believe I overslept shit!" I groaned.

Watergate walked in the room. "Heeyyy, morning boo bear." She greeted me.

"Good morning." I said sitting up.

Watergate had two plates in her hand, she handed me one, and sat the other on her nightstand, beside the bed. She disappeared and came back carrying two glasses and a jug of apple juice.

She sat beside me and kissed me on the cheek. I was hungrier than a runaway slave.

"How ya head feeling boy?" She asked, as we ate and talked.

"I'm decent now." I replied.

"Oh, I know you decent. Mama put that ass to bed last night."

We both busted out laughing.

"Nah, I put you to sleep." I responded.

"Chiillddd…ppllease! You were out in the 3rd round. Nigga this pussy got that whip appeal, and you had a babyface this morning." She boasted laughing.

"Oh, nah, you can't get out on me like that." I said.

"Too late." She squeaked as I came forward.

The covers came down and I realized, I was still naked.

"Um, look at ya little soldier." She teased.

"Man, fuck you." I laughed as I snatched the covers back up.

"That's what we did last night, so now what's new." She responded, being sarcastic. "So, what you gonna do Fox, be my nigga or what?"

"Le' me check this B.J. thin…" I started but was cut off by her.

"I told you I don't fuck wit' no…"

I cut her back off. "Girl just let me find out, so I can burn your ass up."

She started blushing, "Hold up, I gotta go to the bathroom." She said.

As she entered the bathroom her telephone rang. "Fox get that boo." She yelled from the bathroom.

"Hello!" I answered.

"Ooo…who dis?" A girl voice responded.

"This Fox, who dis?" I asked.

The voice turned sexy. "Oh you don't remember me huh?"

"Nah, Joe who dis?" I asked.

"This is Tisha, you 'member you met me and my cousin down on Division Avenue. You paid for our food!"

"Oh yeah, what's happening shorty." I asked.

"Nah what's happening wit' you? What you doing over my cousin's house early in the morning?"

"Nothing...chilling. I accidently fell asleep last night." I lied.

"Yeah, I'll bet you did." She laughed.

"Hey, do you want to speak to Watergate?" I asked.

"Nah, I'm talkin' to you now." She replied.

"Look shorty you barking up the wrong tree." I told her.

"I like this tree." She said.

"Oh yeah." I asked.

"Oooh, yeah." She responded. "Le' me get your number." I gave her my beeper number. "I'ma page you too, don't be faking either." She threatened.

"Yeah, whatever." I said.

"Fox who dat on the phone?" Watergate yelled from the bathroom.

"It's your cousin Tish!" I yelled back.

"Tell her to call me back," she responded.

"A'ight." I replied. "You heard that?" I asked Tisha.

"Yeah, I heard it, I'll see you later." She said then hung up.

I got up and put my clothes on, Watergate came out of the bathroom.

"Boo where are you going?" She asked.

"I got to go home."

"Why don't you stay for a while?" She whined.

"Girl, I'll see you later." I replied.

"Oh, that's how you gonna do it huh…just fuck me and leave me huh?" She was getting angry.

"Nah, you said that shit, I didn't." I answered. "Don't go there with me Watergate."

"Nah, nigga cause you act like you can't stay." She fussed.

"Look I'm coming back later." I told her as I walked passed.

"Nigga, if you don't come back, I'ma come up the Heights and embarrass your ass." She threatened.

"Whatever." I walked down the stairs, while she stayed upstairs.

As I walked toward the door I looked over at the couch.

Her aunt Rita's purse was still sitting on the couch. Rita had stayed out, all night. I hurriedly ran to the purse, opened it, and dumped the contents out.

"Bingo!" I said. I found what I was looking for.

That big ass Ziploc bag of weed. I unzipped the bag, dumped all the weed out, and stuffed the bags in my pockets. I returned about thirty bags just so it wouldn't look that bad. After that, I scooped up everything and put it back in her purse. I quickly put the purse back where it was and headed out the front door.

"Damn that weed was crucial." I mumbled headed for my car.

CHAPTER TWENTY-TWO

I drove up the Heights and parked, I heard it was a big crap game up the hill. So, I decided to go try my hand. I grabbed my hamma and headed towards the game.

When I arrived, all the hustlas was out there. Jabar, Keith, Peter-Rabbit, Dirk, Lil' Feet Kevin, Boo-Boo, Twon, Black Frankie, Snuff, B.J., Domo, Pee-Wee, Ronald, Omar, and so many others, I had to squeeze through niggas to get a glimpse at who was on the dice.

When I looked it was the two big boys going head to head. Jabar and Lil' Feet Kevin, both had a stack of money in front of them.

"Show 'em who da boss...Nina Ross!" Jabar yelled, throwing the dice to the ground.

"We need no sweaters, we need betters! Scared money, don't make no money!" Lil' Feet Kevin yelled.

"Y'all better bet wit' me cause this nine gonna put his ass to sleep, when I bang it." Jabar bragged. "Nine bitch!" He yelled even louder, throwing the dice again. "Woo-wee!"

The dice spun and landed on an eight.

"I'm tellin' y'all get dis money, this bama sweeter than bear meat. If that bitch wink, she'll fuck!" Jabar yelled out.

I decided to bet with him. "I got a hundred say he do it! Anybody want this money." I yelled.

"Nigga you ain't nothing'." Boo-Boo responded to my call out.

"Bet den!" I said.

"It's a bet." He replied.

We gave each other a pound to seal the deal. While we were waiting on Jabar to hit or miss his number. I saw B.J. in the crowd.

"Hey B.J. le' me holla at cha young." I called.

He looked up from the crap game and walked over to me. "What's up Joe?" He asked.

"Man, I just finish fucking the dog shit outta Watergate last night. I punish dat pussy." I told him.

Niggas in ear shot busted out laughing.

"Is that ya bun?" I questioned.

"Nah, I don't fuck wit' that freak ass bitch, I just fucked her. Why?" He asked.

Now that I think back in retrospect I should've kept my fuckin' mouth closed. "Nah, I heard that was your bun a while ago and I wanted to pull you up on game. You know how bitches play things."

"Yeah young I know how them fun..."

"Slaughter house bitches!" Jabar yelled cutting us both off.

Jabar had made his point.

"Le' me get dat paper young!" I hollered over to Boo-Boo.

Boo-Boo handed me the hundred-dollar bill, as Jabar and Lil' Feet Kevin threw more money down and went back at it.

"Place ya bets now!" Jabar yelled.

"Yeah as I was saying." B.J. continued. "Them bitches is funky!"

"I feel ya young." I said.

"A'ight let me get back to the dice game. I got this joint on me, so a nigga gotta watch out for the Bo-Dens."

"A'ight Joe." B.J. said.

We stepped back to the crap game and observed. A couple of minutes later, B.J. excused himself from the game, looking frustrated. I thought it was because he'd loss, so I really didn't pay it any attention. I continued to place my bets, I had won three hundred and fifty dollars, so I was feeling good. I placed a fifty-dollar bet on Kevin and lost. I decided to quit while I was ahead. I gently excused myself from the crowd of dudes.

I started walking back towards my building, for some reason I had an eerie feeling, something was gonna happen that day. I walked past a group of youngin's playing football. I decided to spend some time with them and play. My homegirl Stacy was outside, along with my homegirl Pooh watching her son, Lil' Rob play football.

"Hey Stacy, hold my car keys and joint for me." I requested. I handed her my keys and my gun.

"Hey Fox!" Pooh called out.

"Hey Pooh girl." I spoke back. "Damn Stacy I got a feeling something might happen to me today," I confessed.

"Boy don't say that." Stacy replied looking serious. "Do you want to come to my house and chill?" She offered.

"Nah, I'ma fuck around wit' tha youngin's then go over Southeast to hustle." I told her.

"You sure?" She asked.

"Yeah I'm sure." I answered.

I ran out on the grass to play with the youngin's. Their ages ranged from eight to ten. They were running around laughing as I chased them. Stacy and Pooh looked on admirably as I played with the kids. After the game I had to go take a shower. I had grass stains everywhere and was soaking wet from sweat.

"Hold dat til' I get back." I told Stacy, handing her my hamma as I walked toward my building.

I got to my apartment and headed straight to my room. Big Doris was in her room watching T.V. I took my dirty clothes off and took a shower.

I came out and went to my room, I was feeling refreshed now. I put on a pair of Tommy Hilfiger Nylon sweatpants, a dark grey T-shirt, and a Gortex pullover hoodie. I still felt eerie, so I went inside my mattress and grabbed my Mac-11.

I usually didn't fuck wit' that joint unless I had work call, but it made me feel safe. I strapped it in the inside pocket of my Gortex jacket, just in case I needed it, it would be easy to get to. All I had to do was zip the zipper on the side and there it was, ready to be used. I was feeling better now.

I put on my black Gortex Hi-Tech boots that matched my jacket. I grabbed my money and headed for the door.

****

Once I stepped outside, it was bright, sunny, and slightly windy. But people were outside in T-shirts, shorts, jeans and more. I wanted something to snack on, so I walked to the candy lady at Collen's house.

I bought two packs of dinosaur eggs, some cool ranch Doritos, a snickers bar, and a Hawaiian punch drink. I felt better as I walked toward Stacy's building. Stacy was sitting on the front, she saw how fresh I looked and smiled.

Stacy was a pretty face, slight, chubby broad. She could sing her ass off and she had a son by one of the Go-Go band members from Junkyard.

"Stacy throw them keys and hold that joint." I told her.

Just as Stacy threw my car keys, I saw two male figures walking towards me in black coats. One was pulling out a chrome .45 handgun, the other already had his gun drawn holding it down beside his left thigh. I saw two other figures run behind the building to trap me off.

"Run Nigga…Run!" My own thoughts shouted out.

I don't know how I caught my car keys, but the next thing I knew, I was sprinting as fast as I could past buildings to make it across the street.

I put my keys in my front upper pocket, as I ran. I was running so fast my feet were kicking my ass. I looked back and saw the second dude had ran past the first dude. Looking back caused me to trip over my foot and fall but I was running so fast that when I fell my body weight propelled me to do a frontwards flip. I immediately got up and continued running.

Pop…pow…pow…pop!

I heard the first shots, I was trying to get the Mac out. I had unzipped my side zipper on my jacket, but I had to get safe. There were kids outside playing.

"Get the kids…get them babies in the house!" I yelled as loud as I could.

I looked back once again as I was freeing the Mac-11 from my pocket and I saw him. Everything slowed down as if time itself was slowed down. He stood on the top step and looked both ways before he saw me and took aim.

As he was firing I could see his hamma cock back and spit shells from the side of the gun. Fire exploded from the muzzle, round after round. It's true that sometimes you can see your whole life flash before your eyes.

Because at that moment as time stood still. I started to see memories before my eyes of when I was a kid on up to my teenage years. I even saw things I didn't remember.

*Pop…pop…pop…pow…pow…*the bullets were colliding with my man big Juicy's Cadillac as I zoomed past it.

I pulled out the Mac-11, switched the safety off, and squeezed the trigga at my target. The fully auto burst with a roar as shells spit from the mouth of the gun. I squeezed off at least seventeen shots before a bullet bit into my arm.

"Aargghh…" I yelled as I dropped the gun.

It was too many bullets coming my way. I had to run, so I hauled ass. "Aahh…shit!" I grunted as a bullet bit me in the leg.

Then another one in the right ass cheek. I rounded the corner out of the line of fire of the oncoming bullets. I kept running, blood was pouring down the back of my right thigh and my right calf felt numb.

"Damn this is it…this is it…this is it." I kept screaming inside my head.

No matter what I kept running down the hill towards Kelly Miller field. I didn't want to stop because I thought they were gonna run me down.

I knew if they pursued me, I was as good as dead. The usual routine when murdering someone is that if you shoot them and if they run you chase them down and finish the job.

That's law in these streets. I was a murder waiting to happen, but I had to keep running. I made it all the way down to Kelly Miller field to the basketball court. I had fell numerous times, I saw a girl I knew from around the neighborhood named Kim. She was playing basketball with a dude.

"Hey Kim…Hey Kim!" I weakly called. "Help me!"

"Lil' Fox what's wrong?" She asked worried.

"Maan, some niggas just shot me!" I said.

Kim saw all the blood and started screaming. "Oh my God…Fox."

"Hey slim give me a ride to the hospital." I asked dude.

He was trying to console Kim. "Hold up shorty I gotcha." He said.

He grabbed Kim by the shoulders leading her to his parked car on the side of the basketball court. He opened the passenger side door, seated her, then ran to the driver's side.

"Hey slim." I tried to yell, hopping towards the car as that bitch ass nigga drove off in a hurry.

I hopped across the street and collapsed in an elderly couple's front lawn. I was extremely exhausted and paranoid.

The front lawn I collapsed on belonged to the Green witch. This house had been there since we were kids and we never saw nobody come in or out, in all my years of living in the neighborhood. We would just see an old lady with long grey hair peak out the living room curtains. We would scream it's the Green witch, the Green witch...run! You know how kids imaginations are, but we truly believed it was a witch in that house because we never saw nobody except the grey haired lady.

Now I was laying in the Green witch's front yard, shot, and bleeding profusely. How bad could my luck be.

I'm on the lawn slipping in and out of consciousness. I'd lost a lot of blood and I was feeling weaker. When I opened my eyes to search for the sky.

A beautiful angelic face appeared. It was so magnificently beautiful, it glowed with a bright aura. It was an old woman with beautiful flowing grey hair. She had to be an angel, I thought. Because of the heavenly way she spoke and her gentle loving touch.

"Just lay back now poor, baby. Let Grandma take care of you. You're in good hands!" Her angelic voice spoke to me. "I used to be a registered nurse many, years ago. I hate to see my poor children out here in these streets, getting shot and murdered. I love you all." She said and started crying.

"I've watched y'all run past my house every day and I would peak at y'all just to see y'all smiling faces run off. I've watched you grow up boy." She continued.

I couldn't see nothing, but her face.

"Charlie go call the ambulance while I keep him safe." She hollered.

Who in the hell was Charlie?' I thought.

The old lady kept feeling my head asking me how I felt. She told me to stay awake. She asked me where I was shot at, but I was too weak to answer.

"That's all right baby, I understand save your energy." She whispered. She put my head in her lap and cradled me as if I was a baby. "Jesus you put him here in my arms for a reason. Lord my Savior, don't take this poor baby." She began pleading aloud.

As she was praying, I could hear a car pull up and slam on brakes.

'Damn this is it.' I thought again.

I tried to make her let me go, because I didn't want her to die with me.

"Baby I promise to keep you safe. They gonna have to kill me too." She said.

"Grandma these niggas ain't got no problem wit' that." I wanted to say aloud but couldn't.

My vision was slightly blurred, but I could see dudes get out of a big car with guns in their hands.

"If you gonna kill my baby, then you can just shoot me too." The old lady said to my amazement.

"Nah, ma'am this my man right here. We came to make sure he stay safe." A voice.

I recognized the voice it was my man Sco talking. Then I heard Juicy, Tye, Greg, and Ronald. I couldn't decipher the rest of the voices.

"Put dem thangs up, my husband Charlie just called the ambulance. So, I'm sure the police will be coming as well." She said.

"Yes, ma'am." Sco politely responded.

"Squirrel young is you alright?" Tye asked.

"What happened?" Juicy asked.

"We got the joint you dropped beside Juicy's car." Tye informed.

"They punished Juicy shit." Sco said.

"That joint look like Swiss cheese." Tye retorted.

"Yeah that joint saved your ass, or you would have caught every bullet." Juicy said.

As the sirens approached, the police and the ambulance pulled up. The old lady kissed my forehead before letting me go.

*Beep…beep…beep…*my pager went off. I tried to see the number. Recognized it was Watergate's number.

The pager went flying as Sco smacked it out of my hand. "Nigga you about to damn near die and you worryin' bout who beepin' you. Nigga fuck dat pager. You gotta go to the hospital!" He barked.

They hurried up and put me on the stretcher, while the paramedics cut my sweatpants off, checking to see where I was hit.

The police questioned the old lady. Tye was walking beside the stretcher while the paramedics was lifting me in back of the ambulance.

"Squirrel, man you stayed over that bitch Watergate house last night? Man, young I been told you 'bout dat bitch. I told you…I told you…I told you." Was all I heard from Tye as they put the oxygen mask on my face.

As I faded into oblivion the last face I saw was B.J.'s. I saw his eyes, but I finally got the chance to meet a living angel. The Green witch.

CHAPTER TWENTY-THREE

I was there laid up in D.C. General Hospital unconscious. I had to be transferred due to security purposes. My mother Big Doris didn't want me to reside there, she had saw on the news previously that a man walked in the hospital and shot another man to death after he'd already been shot. D.C. General hospital wasn't secured enough for my safety, so Big Doris had me moved to Howard University Hospital uptown.

My breathing was a slow rhythm. My eyes were closed, I felt the I.V. in my arm as I just laid there. I kept my eyes closed rewinding the past moments of my life. I came to realize that even though I had people around me. I was still lonely as hell.

Why me'? I wondered.

I seemed to get hurt when I least expected it. My anger surfaced out of being hurt. "Fuck it...let it out." I told myself. Tears silently rolled down each side of my eyes.

I felt someone grab my hand and kiss me on the lips.

"Shush," They whispered.

Ole Big Doris, I knew she would come through. I felt the weight of the bed shift as she sat next to me.

"Mama?" I spoke barely above a whisper, my eyes still closed.

"No baby it's me...Keisha."

I slowly opened my eyes to see Keisha's green eyes staring at me, tearfully. Keisha bent down and kissed me again.

"Whatcha doing here?" I asked angrily.

"Baby I been with you the whole time. I got a call and when I heard you had been shot. I grabbed my things and came straight to D.C. General. I met your mother over there, when she had you transferred here. She couldn't make it, so I came up here by myself." Keisha said.

"Maan…where's my mother…where's my men and 'em at?" I questioned.

"Boy I'm the only one that's here and been here. I been here since eleven o-clock p.m. last night. It's what…1 p.m. today. Your mother said she gonna come later, but none of your so-called men or shall I saw boys, been here to check up on you."

"Well, I know they comin'… they drove me to the hospital." I informed her, turning my head to one side looking out the large window.

Keisha grabbed my face and looked directly into my eyes, "Nigga when are you gonna get it in ya thick ass skull of yours. I heard why you got shot Fox." She snapped pissed.

"Maan, my men got my back." I insisted.

"Well where the fuck is your men at now…huh? Don't let them niggas size yo' head up."

"Size what…my men got love for me." I continued.

"Nigga, I love you." Keisha screamed. "I got your muthafuckin' back. That lil' bitch that you 'spose ta have fucked or them fake ass friends of yours don't l…o…v…e…you.

They don't care about you. Who gonna take care of you besides ya mama. Me…that's who. Where they at Fox? Nowhere to be found but look who's here…me." She fussed.

"Why the fuck you leave me then?" I yelled. "Why are you even here? Man, I loved you, Joe. How you gonna carry a nigga like that." I cried out.

"How you gonna just…after all the shit I did for you." I cried harder, stumbling over my words.

"Excuse me is everything all right in here?" A nurse asked peaking her head into the room.

"Yeah, we a'ight, just some family issues." Keisha replied.

"Oh, I'm sorry." The nurse said leaving.

"Because Fox I was pregnant, so I went and had an abortion without speaking with you first. That's why I went away, I couldn't face you. I...I...I didn't think.

I just went and did it once I found out. I knew you would be hurt Fox." Keisha cried. "I killed our baby and now I regret it so much." She sobbed as huge tears poured from her eyes.

I felt like shit, I'd never given her a chance to explain. I grabbed her head and laid it on my chest, as she hugged me and cried more.

"Shush, baby I'm sorry too." I kissed her forehead as we laid there and cried together.

Rumor spread fast about the shooting. There were all kinds of rumors going around. I was dead, I was paralyzed, I had a leg amputated, and more.

Several detectives came to visit me while I was in the hospital, questioning me about who'd shot me.

"Mr. Jonathan Fox, did you see who shot you and do you know why anyone would want to shoot you?" The detective asked.

"Nah, I didn't see nobody, I was too busy running." I replied.

"Have you heard any rumors about who shot you?" The other detective asked.

"Man look how the fuck I'm 'sposed to know who shot me. I am in the hospital and no I don't want to find out who shot me because I'm not doing no snitch shit for no Bo'Dens."

"Well..." the detective looked at his partner. "I guess that seals the case for me." He said.

"Me too." His partner answered.

They gave each other a hi-five and got up to leave.

"I guess you'll tell us who shot you, the next time a bullet hits you in your fuckin' head instead of your ass." The detective insulted.

"Hmmp…a dead man tells no tales." I remarked.

"My point exactly." The detective snapped, as they exited the room.

Keisha had nurtured me back to health, with her support and love. Our bond definitely grew stronger.

She played a major role in my recovery. I had been staying between her and my aunt Tinan's house.

Keisha wouldn't let me out of her sight, but I had to handle my business. It's hard to understand the trauma of being shot and knowing the niggas who shot you. I was about to go all out on a mission. I felt I was invincible now, I'd escaped death twice and lived to tell the stories.

One day when Keisha went around Barry Farms to visit her aunt Peaches. I crept back around my hood. I had on a grey and blue Nautica Sweatshirt, some double sole Timberlands, and a black Skully on my head.

I went to my mother's house and grabbed Snuk's .10mm handgun. It was just beginning to get dark outside. I went and stood in front of Tye's building. Memories flooded my mind, I remembered when six Jamaicans was killed execution style in that very hallway, because of a drug deal gone bad.

The Jokers thought they were going to come to D.C. in Lincoln Heights and setup shot. What they didn't know was that Lincoln Heights didn't tolerate any outsiders.

I remembered hearing the loud bangs of gunfire as guns exploded in the hallways. I stood inside my building peeking through the crack of the door, as the assailants walked away from the scene as if nothing ever happened. I crept to the crime scene to witness blood dripping from the rails onto the steps, and the sick copper smell of fresh blood.

I saw a leg poking out upstairs, I peeked through the railing and saw a bloody hand. I looked up to the fire escape and saw a man with his hands tied behind his back and his brains blown out all over the wall. That was it for me, I had seen enough. I calmly walked back to my building when I heard sirens. That was some gruesome shit, I watched the police and paramedics rush to the scene.

One police officer vomited at the sight of gore. Cameras came rushing to catch a glimpse of the horrific scene. It was the true crime show, City Under Siege. They documented the cities homicides. The killers put their work in. The district always been a place where principal overrides money any day. Niggas catch bodies like colds, I knew I had to put it down like the big homies did. Lincoln Heights never had an outsider to try to set up shop again. It sent a clear message to outsiders.

I snapped back to reality, I had to handle this business another day. Tonight, I wasn't focused on revenge. My mind had wandered to the Green witch. I felt a pang of emotion rush over me. I was very touched at the thought of this woman helping me. So, I decided to go pay here a personal visit, just to let her know, I truly appreciated what she did. I began to walk toward the Green witch's house.

Once I arrived, I walked up to the front door and knocked. I waited for a response, then the door opened. Standing there in the doorway was that same angelic face. When she saw my face, she lit up with a beautiful bright smile that made me return a heartfelt smile.

"Hi...babe come in." She greeted.

"Charlie...look who came to visit us." She called her husband.

"H-how are you doing ma'am?" I greeted her. I reached out to shake her hand.

"No, babe you give me a hug?" She reached out and embraced me.

I returned her hug tightly; a rush of emotions came over me and I started crying. "I…I…just wanted to t…thank you for what…you did for me." I cried.

I pulled back reached in my pocket and grabbed a knot full of money. It was close to two thousand dollars, I looked up into her eyes. She was silently crying, I tried to put the money in her hands.

"Heavens no baby I don't want your money." She refused.

"B…but I want you to have it, to show you that I can't thank you enough. I could…could have died without your help."

"Babe I know you are thankful by just coming down to my house expressing yourself. You all are my neighborhood babies. I watched so many of y'all for years growing up, calling me the Green witch.

If I lose one of you I can't get you back, but if I lose money I can always get it back." She said soothingly. "My name is Gloria, and this is my husband of thirty-eight years Charlie."

Her husband walked into the living room. "Hey son how're ya doin?" He asked.

"I'm straight." I said wiping the tears away from my eyes.

"Have a seat," Ms. Gloria offered as she folded my hand around the money.

Her living room was painted a very light brown. The furniture was white, and she had old family pictures and a lot of little antique ornaments around.

It was a very warm place, I sat down and the three of us talked for hours. She cooked us a meal and we had baked cookies for dessert. I never felt more welcomed and more comfortable in my life. She showed me pictures of her and her husband when they were younger. She was super beautiful and classy.

She beamed with pride when I told her, just like wine ya get fine wit' time. Charlie her husband chuckled, all their four children were grown and moved out on their own.

I told jokes and cracked them up with laughter. It had gotten to be late, so I had to excuse myself.

"Boy times flies when you're having a good time." Charlie said.

"Yes, it does." I agreed.

"But if you all would excuse I have to get going. Maybe we can continue this another time." I suggested.

"Anytime." Ms. Gloria squealed, smiling with tears in her eyes.

I walked over to her and hugged her tight.

"Baby you be safe now, so you can come back and tell me some more stories and jokes." She whispered. "You're welcomed here anytime. You just don't know how happy you made me today. I haven't had a good laugh like that in years. Thank you, babe." Ms. Gloria said. "I know the Lord works in mysterious ways. He sent you back to me like fruit give seeds back to the earth. Be good now baby." Ms. Gloria continued finally letting me go.

I walked over to her husband Charlie and shook his hand in a firm grip. I looked him in his eyes, then told him. "Thank you sir, for everything."

Charlie nodded his head in a silent agreement and appreciation. I said my goodbyes then exited the front door.

As I was leaving I looked back to see Ms. Gloria watching me out the living room curtains. She was beautiful, no longer the Green witch, but a beautiful angel.

CHAPTER TWENTY-FOUR

Over the past few weeks, niggas were getting dropped like flies around the Heights. It was as if a ghost reappeared. I had stepped my murder game up. Any nigga who affiliated with my enemies died.

I was back with a vengeance. Snuk tried to calm me down, but to me he was getting soft on me. Being real he just tried to guide me in the right direction before I got jammed up, either in a wooden box or pacing four corners. But I wasn't stuntin' what he was talkin' 'bout. I had gotten shot and niggas was gonna pay.

I punished damn near their whole crew. This beef was different from Mohammad. I still had to get slim, but for now I had to worry about the niggas who were closer to my head.

Some niggas that was perpin', just got hot rocks off the muscle. The shit was getting hectic, I was trying to flush B.J. ass out of the hole he was hiding in.

One night I waited in the bushes for him to come in front of his building. I waited in those pissy ass bushes all fuckin' night. Then finally he got out of a car, I could see him through the bushes. He was coming towards the apartment building where I was hiding, I moved a little to loosen my muscles in my body. I've been there all night crouched down so my joints and muscles had stiffened.

The bush must have slightly moved and caused B.J. to stop walking and took a step backwards.

I knew if I didn't get him then, he would go back into hiding. Just when he was about to run, I raised up and started firing.

P-pow...pop...pop...pow... the gun roared as I fired away at him.

I had a P-89 twenty-one shot Ruger. B.J. ran jumped on the hood of a car, slid to the street, and proceeded to run at top speed. I ran a little awkwardly because of my joints being stiff. I tried to chase him, but he was too fast.

One of the shots must have hit him because I saw him jerk forward violently, but he kept his balance and kept running down the street through a dark cut. I knew he was going to Wayne-Wayne's house to get help and maybe a gun if he wasn't seriously damaged. I ran in the dark to an alley and got ghost. I'd catch his bitch ass later.

"Damn this nigga got away." I spat angrily.

Heat was on, niggas in every direction was trying to give me free coke, guns, and all kinds of shit for allegiance. I was hip to these artificial alliances.

Truth be told, these bitch ass niggas was scared to death, because word had gotten out how I was putting in work wit' the hammas.

My name was ringing in the whole Northeast area. So, whoever had a nigga like me on their team had more strength and the more niggas would fear them. I wasn't gonna get used like no pond. Niggas really wanted protection, but I had my own problems to deal with.

Drama was really boiling, I had come to find out, I did hit B.J., but it was only a flesh wound. He went and told Wayne-Wayne, another one of Lincoln Heights cold-blooded murderers. Me and Wayne-Wayne came up together around Capers Southeast D.C. But as we moved to Lincoln Heights our friendship had somewhat drifted apart.

Now he was an enemy, Snuk was beefing with Wayne-Wayne to because Wayne-Wayne shot Snuk's partner Kevin outside in broad daylight in front of everybody over some heated word exchange.

Wayne-Wayne wasn't to be fucked with, he came from a bloodline of killer soldiers. From his father Big Wayne to all of his uncles, especially the infamous one leg Go-Go. He was a legend for going hard in those streets and getting money.

Wayne-Wayne was groomed by him, Wayne-Wayne busted his hamma so much, they nicked named him John Wayne.

But anyway, the drama was getting so heated that Wayne-Wayne came to see me personally. We had previously had a shootout a week before down on Division Avenue. I was coming out of the carryout while Wayne-Wayne and some dudes was on the other side of the street.

As I came out the store, we saw each other and locked eyes. After that…all hell broke loose. We exchanged gunfire for a second. I found an escape route by Clay Terrance Creek and bolted towards it. No gunfire followed, but that was too damn close.

Now Wayne-Wayne came to visit me, I was in my mother's house watching T.V. When I heard somebody call my name outside of the window.

"Hey, Squirrel…"

I looked out the window to see that it was Wayne-Wayne. I dropped back in the window and crawled to my room to retrieve my gun.

I thought it was on, my heart was pounding in my chest as fear gripped me. He saw the way I ducked out the window and ran to the playground in front of my building that we call, the Maze. It had high and low walls for protection in case a person was shooting.

Wayne-Wayne knew the type of mentality I had, I'd kill a muthafucka who violated. I'd bust that hamma anywhere when needed.

"Hey youngin'…hey youngin. Hold…hold…hold, Joe." He yelled as I came to the front of my building door, peaking out, aiming my Glock .40 towards the maze walls where he was.

"Squirrel, I ain't here to rock youngin. I'm here to holla at cha…straight up," Wayne-Wayne said. "Look," he said as he ejected a shell from the head of a massive chrome .45 then ejected the clip.

Wayne-Wayne pulled the trigga to show that the gun wasn't loaded. Then he lifted his shirt and turned around in a .360 motion to show that he wasn't carrying a second gun.

When he lifted his shirt, I noticed he had a bullet proof vest on.

"Youngin' we family slim. I come to talk to ya for real." Wayne-Wayne yelled.

I knew Wayne-Wayne, he'd always been a man of his word, so I stepped out of the building. Wayne-Wayne came walking towards me, my heart was still beating fast, but humor was something we prided our lives on in the hood.

"Damn, young what's up?" Wayne-Wayne asked.

"Whatcha mean what's up…you know the deal." I responded.

"That's what I came to talk to you about. We can't kill each other Squirrel…we grew up together, plus we homies."

I just stood there because Wayne-Wayne had a valid point.

"Squirrel, I was fucked up you busted off on me down Division Ave, young!"

"Nah, Joe I saw you reach Wayne," I said.

"I saw you reach first Squirrel." He replied.

"Look we both reached and dumped off, but at least one of us didn't get hit."

"Yeah Joe." He responded.

"Dig I got a lot of love for you and your brother. Let's squash this shit like gentlemen." Wayne-Wayne offered. "Niggas want us to kill each other off because we the strength of the hood." He continued.

"Yeah I can feel you on that one." I said.

"Maan...tell your brother don't shoot at me and I won't shoot at him. But me and his man Kevin got a beef for life because I dumped them hot balls in his ass."

"Dig whenever my brother come around I'ma let you sort that out." I replied.

"Deal...wit' me, but to me everything is squashed. Damn you tried to punish my son-son B.J.," Wayne-Wayne said.

"Yeah, you know niggas wit' him shot me joe." I told him.

"But B.J. told me you started the beef." This was news to me.

"Man, how the fuck did I start the beef?" I asked.

"Young...B.J. came up the honey comb hide out crying saying that you robbed him at a crap game."

"Man...stop welling youngin." I raised my voice in disbelief.

"Man, I walked up to the crap game and told him that I had just finished fuckin' the dog shit outta that bitch from 58th, Watergate. Youngin' acted like he wasn't trippin', but then he got up and rolled out from the game. I thought he lost his money." I told Wayne-Wayne.

"Come now." Wayne-Wayne said also in disbelief. "You mean all this stupid shit is behind a funky ass bitch! That's why Lil' punk was all crying and shit." Wayne-Wayne said.

"I can't believe youngin' lied like that on me. I thought I was keeping it real."

"Man, I'ma fuck dis nigga ass up when he come home." He said. "Nigga done got smashed behind this girl ass shit he pulled."

"Whatcha mean when he come home?" I asked.

"Oh, B.J. and my uncle got locked up for an attempt on the police last night.

The police were chasing them and B.J. started shooting out the car window to slow them down, but the car transmission gave out and they got caught. He gonna go down Oak Hill and be back in a couple months because he is a juvie.

"My uncle got bread, so he'll find a paid lawyer that'll eat that case."

"Damn Joe." I said in amazement. "They were probably on their way to do a drive by."

"I had to squash our beef because you're a real nigga Squirrel. That shit ain't for us, ya feel me?"

"Yeah I feel you." I said.

"Plus, I kept it gangsta, you could have snitched on a nigga, but you didn't. That's the type of shit I respect." He said.

"Real niggas do real things." I said.

"Youngin' I love you," Wayne-Wayne said as he embraced me in a hug.

I embraced him back, this is what men do, we talk it out. A lot of deaths could have been avoided. If a lot of dudes in the city would have put their egos aside and talked like me and Wayne-Wayne did. A lot of dudes would still be living today.

I'll always respect Wayne-Wayne for that. Now that was gangsta. I learned to never be afraid of your enemies the worse they could do was kill you.

CHAPTER TWENTY-FIVE

Sandman took a trip out of town, so I was on the block grinding until my knees were sore. I decided to go in the house to chill and play with my little sister. I came in the house to find Mickey ass in the kitchen frying a hamburger, high as a kite, singing off tune with a lit cigarette hanging from his mouth.

"Bo…de…bo…wop…ta…wop…ta…wop." He sang off key in between nodding in and out.

'Fuck that singing, I wanted my bread. I finally caught up wit' dis nigga'. I thought.

I peeked around the corner towards Big Doris's room. She was laying down with my little sister.

"Okay, perfect." I mumbled.

I went to my room, closed the door, and pulled out my cell phone. I called Snuk, his phone rang two times then he picked up.

"Hello?" He said.

"Yeah what's up bro?" I asked.

"Shit out here trying to chase this paper." He replied.

"Bet ya know the bama in the kitchen cookin' I'm 'bout to whup dis nigga 'bout my money Joe."

"Before you put the knuckles on him, hold up I'm 'round the corner. I'm bout to come around that joint now." Snuk said.

"A'ight I'ma unlocked the door." I whispered.

We both hung up, I had put my plot in motion. Snuk wanted to whup Mickey anyway, so, I just invited him to my party. I eased back in the kitchen.

Mickey was nodding hard, this bama cigarette ash was long and still intact that I don't how it didn't break off. The hamburger was burnt to a crisp. Mickey was still holding the handle of the frying pan as if he was still cooking. This shit was amusing, how dope fiends held their balance in a nod.

"Mickey." I yelled.

"Um...hmmm." He jumped out of his nod and began turning over the burnt, crisp hamburger as if it wasn't ready.

Mickey was so high he didn't realize, he'd burnt the damn muthafucka.

"Gawd damn shorty, you tryna kill a muthafucka?" He asked.

"Nah, nigga I'm here to collect my money. You been ducking a nigga like I'm five-o, where's my loot. I need that." I said.

"Shawty didn't...I tell yo..." Mickey started but nodded off again.

I reached over cut the stove off and lightly pushed him. "Mickey!" I yelled.

"I told you I'ma get that to you when I cash my income tax return." He lied.

"Nigga stop bojanglin' you high as shit right now." I said.

Just then Snuk walked up behind me.

"Shawty, what da fuck is you...the IRS?" Mickey responded sarcastically.

"Nah, nigga he the repo man and he come to collect his shit." Snuk said over my shoulder.

Mickey woke up when he heard Snuk's voice.

"Man, get my little brother money up nigga...now...tonight." Snuk demanded.

"Dig it youngsta, I'ma hit ya off when I get it. I ain't finna break my neck to cash my check." Mickey said as he tried to squeeze past us.

"Nah, Joe!" I pushed him back into the kitchen.

I knew he was trying to make it to Big Doris's room for safety. Me and Snuk both knew that if he made it to Big Doris's room my chance would be zero in getting my money or beating his ass. Big Doris was this nigga only protection.

I didn't give a fuck that he was my little sister's father, if Big Doris saved him, the whole house getting an ass whupping.

Me and my brother was like two bad little cubs picking a fight.

"Gawd damn shawty, what you want me to do?" Mickey said while scratching his right ass cheek.

"This is what I want you to do. Take this ass whupping then." I said as I jabbed him in the face with a one, two, combo punch.

I hit Mickey straight in his mouth.

"Aaahh…Doris!" This bitch ass nigga screamed, trying to draw a tip.

Snuk rushed in the kitchen and it was on. Snuk punched him on the right side of his jaw and dropped him. I kicked Mickey head back into the cabinets making some dishes fall. While Snuk punched away, Mickey fell over and curled up in a fetal position trying to protect his now bleeding head and face.

I saw that his ribs were exposed, so I bent down and punched him in the ribs as hard as I could I heard a snap.

"Aarrgghhh…" Mickey groaned.

"Bitch ass nigga shut the fuck up! Where is my muthafuckin' money?" I barked as I continued to brutally beat him.

Snuk got behind him and put the choke hold on him.

"Aaahhhh…!" Mickey was gasping trying to breathe.

"Go in his pockets Squirrel…check this nigga pockets!" Snuk said.

I stopped swinging and went in Mickey's front pockets. I found a wad of hundred-dollar bills. Mickey was struggling wilding now.

"Pat this nigga down…fuck that." Snuk grimaced as he was choking Mickey.

I pulled Mickey pants down, this muthafucka didn't have on no drawers. He was swinging commando. I grabbed a spoon and was getting ready to probe him. Mickey's eyes grew big as soccer balls.

"Nooo…Sq…" he tried to say as Snuk continued choking him.

I threw the spoon away and went to his shoes. I took them off, that bama feet was kicking like Bruce Lee. But I hit the jackpot, there was more hundred-dollar bills stuffed in the bottom of each sock.

"Fuck that go in this nigga ass." Snuk hollered. "That's where dope fiends keep the real money."

I grabbed the spoon again, Mickey started bucking like a horse. I cringed my face as I looked at his nakedness. I advanced on him and bent down. I felt a sharp sting in the middle of my back.

"God dammit…get off him…get off him!" Big Doris screamed.

I jumped like a cat on the top of the table, at the sound of her voice. Niggas got to understand my mama whup ass like she got the Holy Ghost in her. Snuk used Mickey's body as a shield as Big Doris was swinging the broom stick frantically.

"Mama dis nigga owe me money, why you taking up for him?" I said.

"I don't give a fuck…y'all don't come in my house disrespecting me! This my house God damnit. I pay tha God damn bills in here." Big Doris yelled, steady swinging the broom stick.

I looked Snuk silently told him he was on his own because I'm getting the fuck outta here, with this woman swinging this stick like a mad Chinese.

Snuk's eyes said the same thing, I got hit again on my elbow, I screamed like a bitch at the pain that shocked my arm.

I faked to the right then to the left, then bolted pass Big Doris. She wasn't fast enough to catch me with another hit.

"You little muthafucka!" Big Doris yelled as I sprinted to the living room out of harms way.

My little sister Poo-Pee was standing in her doorway in her cute Minnie Mouse pajamas crying. I rushed over and kissed her little rosy cheeks.

"Go back to bed for me, I'll bring you some candy tomorrow." I whispered to her.

She nodded, then ran and jumped in her little bed happy. Just then I saw Snuk dragging Mickey towards the door. Mickey must have thought I had left out of the house because now he was fake trying to fight back. But Snuk still had a firm grip on the choke hold.

Snuk dragged Mickey to the front door while Big Doris was trying to figure out how she could get a good swing in. I saw her back in the kitchen, so I knew what that meant. She was going to get a frying pan.

I quickly reacted, I ran to the front door, and opened it. Snuk hurriedly dragged Mickey through the threshold. As Snuk dragged Mickey outside into the hallway. I punched Mickey in the mouth knocking one of his rotten teeth out.

Blood was everywhere, we could hear Big Doris coming so me and Snuk threw Mickey down the flight of steps. He tumbled like a rag doll.

We both descended the steps just in time.

Big Doris came to the door with a big ass butcher knife and a big black skillet frying pan. We were at the bottom of the steps looking up at our mother's angry face. She looked back at us and threw the frying pan at us.

We ducked out of the hallway as the frying pan disintegrated into small chunks of pieces.

Mickey was laying at the bottom of the steps out cold. I peeked back in the building and saw Big Doris staring at me. I hurried up and ran back in the building and kicked Mickey in the head with my boots.

"You black little muthafuckin' bastard!" Big Doris yelled. "That's anough God damnit…thats anough. Get the fuck on, before somebody call the police!" Big Doris continued screaming.

Me and Snuk jogged across the street. I reached in my pocket and gave Snuk half of the money I took from Mickey. We hugged then parted ways. That's fucked up I had to do Ole Mickey's funny as like that, but the nigga did it to himself.

I was angrier at Big Doris for taking his fuckin' side. We were her sons. I jumped in my car and drove towards Keisha's house.

I stayed up Keisha's house until things cooled off. Mickey nor Big Doris didn't tell on us, but I wanted to give them some time alone. So, he could heal in peace, me and Keisha began to argue frequently. I came in Keisha's house one day, looking for my black leather motorcycle jacket. I couldn't find it. I searched the house from top to bottom.

I asked Keisha and she acted like she didn't know where it was. Then all of a sudden, I thought about Louise, Keisha's mother. I walked into the smoked filled kitchen, that smelled like straight raw. Louise and her boyfriend Lawrence's eyes were big and gloomy.

"Hey Louise." I called her.

"Huh baby?"

"Where did you get the money to fill ya lungs up?" I asked.

"Fuck is you my daddy...nigga you in my house and you respect me." She spat back.

"That wasn't my question Louise and I mean no disrespect at all." I replied.

"Well, boy don't ask questions in my house. If any muthafucking thang I do tha' asking around this bitch!"

Right then I knew that bitch had sold my brand-new leather jacket. She sold some other things in the house as well that I'd brought, but I wasn't tripping off that I wanted my jacket.

I walked outside to keep from going off. I couldn't believe this bitch, after all the nice shit I'd done for her and her house. Fuck that I wanted my jacket. I walked to my car, got my gun, and walked down to 37th Place.

"Where you going, Fox?" Keisha yelled.

I ignored her. I reached the parking lot of hustlas. As I walked everybody looked directly at me. This was one of the most dangerous, deadliest, neighborhoods in Washington D.C. I walked right into a killer's nest.

I made an emotional move that was bad on my behalf. I could see the grimaces of resentment starting to form on their faces.

"No nuts…no Glory." I told myself. "Excuse me men." I said as I walked toward the crowd of dudes. "My name Fox, I'm Green eyed Keisha's boyfriend. I'm from Lincoln Heights."

"Yeah so what's up?" One dark-skinned grimy looking dude asked.

"Did Keisha's mother bring a brand-new leather jacket down here and sell it?" I asked.

"What if she did?" A brown-skinned dude asked.

"The bitch stole my jacket and I'm…"

"Look homie." The brown-skinned nigga said cutting me off. "We don't do refunds.

"I'm tryna get my jacket back." I said.

"Like I said, we don't do refunds. Your issue ain't wit' us. Ya issue is wit' her. Don't check the pimp…check tha hoe." He continued.

Laughter broke between the crowd of dudes. I came back to my senses and realized, I was trapped, and he was right. What the fuck was I trippin' off.

"You know what slim, you're right. I got to respect that." I said to him humbly.

"Dig my name, Yummy, Fox and you can get ya jacket back for double the price I paid for it. I paid some slight shit for it, but if you give me three hundred you can get that joint back."

The hairs on the back of my neck raised up. I could feel the tension start to cloud the air. My trigga finger was itching.

"Naw, you can keep that joint. My bad Slim, that's on me." I said trying to find a way out. I wasn't scared though. I was just paranoid because

I didn't know where the shot was going to come from. I didn't want to put my hands in my pocket. That was an automatic death penalty in this hood being an outsider.

"Yeah, I know it was your bad…your beef need not to come this way, but to that bitch!" Yummy said.

"Man, who that y'all talking too?" A voice said coming through the crowd of dudes. Mike appeared from the crowd. "Damn Lil' Fox whatcha doin' down this end? Don't cha know you're in da wrong territory, which means you're out of bounds." Mike said with a wicked grin on his face.

He had the look of a cat knowing that the mice were trapped.

"Mike you know this dude?" The dark-skinned dude asked him.

"Yeah this Lil' Fox…Big Fox little brother from Lincoln Heights."

"Oh yeah, I heard about cuz and 'em." One light-skinned dude said. "So that's youngin' huh? We was…"

Mike cut him off abruptly with a stern look, "Peep dis Lil' Fox don't bring that drama round dis joint." He said.

"Whatcha talkin' bout Joe?" I asked.

"You know what I'm talkin' 'bout…play pussy and get fucked slim. You got me twisted. Fox you know the muthafuckin' streets talk nigga. I'ma just leave it at that, now see ya way back up da street!" Mike snarled.

I knew what Mike was talking about, I still had Mohammad to worry about. If Mike keep jumping out there sooner or later, I'ma have to put him back in his place.

CHAPTER TWENTY-SIX

I made it back up to Keisha's house safely. I was stressed and didn't know how to shake it. My head was hurting so, I laid down on the couch. I was still mad at Keisha for letting her mother swipe my jacket. I was going to give the jacket to Keisha anyway. That's why I was so mad. Keisha came and sat down beside me on the couch.

"Are you alright?" She asked.

"Naw, my head throbbing." I replied.

"Here take these two aspirins." She instructed.

I sat up and threw the pills in my mouth. Keisha went and brought me back a glass of water. I drank the water, burped, then laid down.

While Keisha was talking to me I dozed off to sleep. I was dreaming that someone was trying to cut my pants pockets and steal my coke and money. I opened my eyes to realize it wasn't a dream.

Louise was actually trying to cut a line below my pants pockets, so she could cut my coke and money out. I shook my drowsiness off and grabbed her hand that gripped the pocket knife.

"Louise what the fuck is you doing!" I snapped.

"Nigga shut the fuck up...you gonna give me dis coke!" Louise was geeking like shit.

Pipe heads are some crafty creatures when they get to knicken like a chicken.

I tried to remove Louise's hand from my pocket, but man she had an incredible death grip. I couldn't believe how strong this skinny ass woman was. I tried to pry her hand away with some strength. Her hand would not budge.

"Louise I'm telling you now get the fuck off my pocket!" I barked.

"Telling me what…nigga you gonna give me some of dis coke or I'ma take it all," Louise said.

I couldn't believe this shit. A fuckin' pipe head trying to strong arm rob me…me out of all people. Fuck it this was no different from the rest.

Smack! I punched her in the eye.

"Aargghh…" Louise yelled.

Smack…Smack… I punched her again and again, Louise wouldn't let my pocket go. I forced my way up off the couch.

I grabbed the back of Louise's hair and repeatedly punched her until I busted her left eye and nose. I held her head all the way back, so the blood could go up her nose. She finally let my pocket go.

"Aww muthafucka…you done hit ole Louise…now I gotta cut cha," Louise said with a deranged look in her eyes.

"Laawrence…get my big knife…this muthafucka done hit me…I'ma cut'cha boy!" Louise hollered.

Just then Keisha walked in the living room.

"Oh my God ma, what happened to your face?" Keisha panicked.

"Dat muthafuckin' boy broke all my face bones…I think my face ain't here no more…I can't feel it." Louise said all dramatic and shit.

Louise was lunchin' good as it gets.

"Fox you hit my mother?" Keisha snapped eyeing me.

"Man look at my muthafuckin' pockets Keisha. I woke up and she had a pocket knife trying to cut my coke and money out. I told her a rack of times to let go. She even tried to bite me, Joe. What the fuck am I 'posed to do…let her strong a nigga? You got me fucked up…I ain't going out like that. She already cuffed the leather jacket I was gonna let you have. Man fuck this shit…I'm outta dis joint!" I barked.

"Bitch I'ma kill you!" Louise hollered as she charged me wit' a knife.

I ran out the front door with Louise on my heels chasing me. I hopped the stairs as if I was flying. I broke the entrance of the building to outside.

To my surprise this bitch was still on my heels. To be a crackhead she was pretty swift. I kept running, but she kept at me with the knife. I reached my car and ran around it. She kept following me around and around my car. Now spectators started to gather around watching the drama unfold.

"Bitch I'ma kill you!" Louise yelled.

"Louise I'm telling you…let it go! Let the knife go!" I warned.

"Fuck you bitch!" Louise yelled.

"Somebody get this crazy bitch!" I yelled out.

"Oh, I'ma show you how crazy this is bitch when I plant this knife in ya ass!" she continued.

"Man fuck this!" I mumbled pulling out my Glock .40. "Look ain't running no more." I told Louise pointing the gun at her.

"Oh, you gonna shoot me now? Shoot then!" She mocked.

Damn this lunchin' ass bitch askin' for it. *Boom!* The gun roared as I shot beside her.

"Aahh…shit!" Louise screamed hysterically.

That seemed to capture her full attention. Louise started to back up quickly. The knife dropped out of her hand as fear seized her.

"Baby…Louise sorry!" She said in a pathetic little voice that aggravated me. I was really pissed off now.

"Bitch get the fuck on somewhere…I should kill your dirty, stankin' ass! After all the things I done for you! Bitch do a magic trick and disappear!"

Boom! I fired another round.

Louise turned around and sprinted as fast as she could. The crowd of gawkers dispersed. I hopped in my car, started the ignition, and sped off.

"Fuck this shit!" I spat angrily.

Once again, every time a nigga thinks he doing good the shit turn out bad.

As I drove back around the Heights. I thought about my life, I was only fifteen years old, but had been through more shit than the average man.

I made it back around the way, parked in the only available parking space I could find, which was a little way up the street from my building. I got out and started walking towards my building.

It was calm outside and the neighbors were focused on their daily routines…which was to come outside and talk shit about and to anybody who'd listen. I was engrossed in my thoughts.

"Hey youngin!" I heard a voice in the distance.

That eerie feeling rushed over me, as suddenly everything outside went silent. I turned slightly just to see a white Pontiac speeding towards the side of me.

A dude in a black Ski mask was bracing himself on the passenger side door. He was positioning himself to shoot. I didn't have time to see the driver because my Air Force Ones down shifted to fifth gear as I broke into a sprint.

*Flop…plop…plop…plop…*the gun roared as shots knocked out car windows, trying to embrace me. I ran and jumped over a wall, slid down a little hill, caught my balance, and kept breaking fast. The hot rocks continued to follow my pursuit.

I didn't want to run towards my building just in case I got shot. I didn't want Big Doris to relive that moment again or maybe witness something even worse. I didn't have time to reach for my hamma because these niggas meant business.

I ran past my man Ronald full speed. I saw the look on Ronald's face it was pure fear. He thought he'd be hit in the cross fire. The shots were coming faster, I recognized the sound of the gun. It must have been a Glock.

I tried to turn a corner towards the cut, I slid and fell. The apartment window in front of me exploded in tiny shards of glass. Me falling might have saved my life, my hand was cut and bleeding, but I didn't give a fuck.

Squeeeerrkkkk!

The tires squealed as the car raced off. I found my way into a building hallway. My nerves were shaking badly as I had flashbacks of the first two attempts on my life. I frantically searched myself to see if I was hit. Luckily those was a bad shot. I noticed that my gun was missing.

I must have dropped it when I was running. I calmed myself down and walked out the building. I was still breathing slightly heavy. As I walked passed the corner where I slipped and fell. I noticed my gun laying by the wall, I walked over and picked it up. I was so frustrated that I carried it in my hand.

"You a'ight Squirrel?" Ronald asked me.

"I'm straight Young." I replied.

"Put the hamma up young, them jokers gone. They were in a white Pontiac." He informed.

"No shit Sherlock." I snapped frustrated.

"Damn Squirrel, who were them bamas? Joe you just got shot 'bout a month and a half ago. You got so much beef that a nigga can't stand next to you."

I just looked at Ronald indifferently, he was right it was time to get to the bottom of this shit.

"Did you see any of them jokers faces?" I asked Ronald.

"Nah the shooter had on a ski mask, but the driver was a light-skinned dude wit' a short tapered haircut."

Mohammad. I thought. He got a nigga to dump off at me.

"I'ma kill this bitch ass nigga. I'ma flip that nigga strip." I mumbled under my breath angrily.

I heard sirens in the distance, I had to go.

"Holla at cha, Ronlo." I told Ronald as I fast walked toward my building.

****

I had to give it to him, this nigga Mohammad was on top of his game. The coward ass nigga was good at hide and seek. I had been looking for him for weeks, he'd pop up then lay low.

Tonight, there was a party we heard about on 49th Place, down the street from Lincoln Heights. The word was that all the young bunnies was going to this party. Niggas know how the Heights love to party-hardy, with the young ladies. I put on a pair of all black Air Nikes, a pair of black jeans, and a grey and black sweat shirt. 49th Place was right down the street, so I took a .380 caliber hand gun.

I wasn't expecting no drama, because 49th Place is damn near in Lincoln Heights. It was one street down, if I did run into any problems I had the gun as an equalizer. I secured the gun in my pocket. Snuk was in the living room watching T.V. when I came out of my room prepping my attire.

"Shawty where you going?" He asked.

"Oh we 'bout to skate down 49th Place to a party. I heard some bad bitches gonna be down that joint partyin'." I replied.

"There you go wit' that playa shit." Snuk teased. "What happened to Keisha? Y'all still beefin'?"

"I don't really know, I'm just giving her some space."

"Squirrel you a funny muthafucka. When you told me how you whupped her mother I died laughing." Snuk laughed.

"It is what is it. That bitch kirked out and tried to strong arm a nigga."

Snuk burst out laughing. He was laughing so hard, tears were running down his face.

"Woo-wee that's some funny shit. I could see the look on your face now." Snuk said still laughing.

"Well you should have saw the look on that bitch face when I punched her in the eye."

Snuk burst out laughing again, he fell on the floor, balled up crying laughing. We made a joke out of me whupping Keisha's mother, Louise.

"Peep game, I'm 'bout to bounce down tha street. Whatcha doing here anyway Snuk?" I asked.

"A nigga needed a break from tha block. Tesa getting on my fuckin' nerves. Pipe heads, all God damn noise, everything." Snuk explained.

"I feel ya…I'll see ya when I get back." I gave Snuk some dap and walked out the door.

"Man, what took you so long?" Tye asked as I exited my building.

Him and a group of my homeboys were waiting on me.

"Y'all fresh!" I said.

Everybody gear was fresh and well groomed. Lincoln Heights youngins always stayed fly. Especially Ronald and Black Mike. Those two niggas always tried to make a fashion statement.

"A'ight let's roll." I said as we started to walk down the street towards 49th Place.

When we arrived at the building we could hear the music thumping from the third-floor apartment. We entered the building and went to where the party was at.

Tye knocked on the door and we waited, the door opened to the face of an old brown-skinned lady. The music rushed out in a loud roar.

"Come in…come in." She smiled.

We entered the apartment and to my amazement there were no girls. There was only young children. I looked around and there wasn't no sign of adults to come. There were some cheese puffs in a big red bowl and some sodas on ice in a trash can. This shit didn't seem right.

"Hey y'all I'm about to skate from this joint." I yelled to be heard over the loud music.

"Man, for what, the bitches ain't here yet." Tye hollered.

"It don't look like broads playing this spot." I said.

"Let's wait and see." Ronald suggested.

"Greg ask that lady when everybody's gonna show up." I instructed.

I looked around, this was a kiddie party. I watched Greg approach the woman and began talking. I couldn't hear what he was saying, because the music was loud. But I saw her keep looking at me then averting her eyes away nervously. That caught my attention, then the lady started biting her nails.

Greg came back over to me as the lady went into a back room.

"Joe what that bitch say?" I asked Greg

"She said she just called everybody on their way!" Greg responded. "Let's chill until everybody come."

"Fuck that, that bitch gave me the goosebumps." I grumbled.

I was getting the fuck up out of there. I was starting to feel claustrophobic. This stupid ass nigga Greg just wanted to party.

I wasn't that pressed to party. I went to everybody and told them let's bounce. Everybody reluctantly agreed. We exited the party, as we descended the hallway steps and exited the building. I noticed there were a few dudes out in the front building who wasn't there when we first arrived.

I recognized one light brown-skinned, medium height dude named Chris. He was originally from Maryland, but he hung in D.C. I wandered what the hell he was doing on this side of town.

"Hey Fox, what's happenin'?" Chris greeted as he came forward.

Chris had on a whole Gucci sweat suit, and some Timberland boots. He sported a black wave cap. He had a bottle of Moet in his left hand. He walked towards me and threw his right arm around my shoulder.

As I was walking to leave around the side of the building, Chris walked to me with his arm still around my shoulder.

"What up nigga?" Chris said in a drunken slur.

"Shit what's up wit' you?" I asked. "What you doing on this end?"

"Ah nothin' came to holla at some people."

"What people is them?" I questioned.

Just then I noticed, Chris was trying to guide me towards the backside of the building with his hip lightly. I peeped it was dark to my right where he was trying to guide me. I didn't smell any alcohol on his breath.

I peeped at the Moet bottle and it was damn near full. This shit was a set up the whole time. I took Chris's arm from around my shoulder, quick and forcibly. As I turned out of his grasp, all in one motion he spun ducking in the other direction as a figure appeared out of the dark backside of the building raising a gun.

I saw Tye, Ronald, Greg, and Black Mike break into a run in slow motion. The figure fired at me as I was back peddling, getting my .380 out of my pocket.

I fell to the ground on my back, as he fired away, and started returning fire with the .380. I only had thirteen shots. This fuck boy nigga was scared to death. He turned and proceeded to run in a sprint to make it around the corner.

When he touched the corner, I could see in the light that it was that nigga Mohammad. I basically just fired shots to get the nigga off my back. It worked this bitch ass nigga couldn't aim the gun for shit.

Out of all the shots I was grazed in my right arm, but it was no biggie just a flesh wound. I jogged up the street to my house. The homey Domo was out front when I ran up holding my arm.

"Fox what's up young?" Domo asked frantically.

"That bitch ass nigga dumped off at us down 49th."

"Who?" Domo asked.

"Mohammad coward ass! That nigga gots ta get it!" I said walking towards my building.

Domo followed me, this bama was perpin' like shit. He really was trying his hand. It all came back to me, he set up the fake party at a crackhead apartment.

Knowing that we would come, so they could trap us. Well…me actually, when the bitch called somebody, she called him to inform him that I came. That's why she kept peeking at me. Chris was Mohammad's man I had put it together. That's why he was around there. It was also Mohammad that shot at me in the white Pontiac.

I came in the house, Snuk was at the door.

"I heard some shots…what the fuck…you bleedin' Squirrel!" Snuk said shocked.

"Yeah don't trip it's only a flesh wound. The bullet went straight through." I replied.

"Who did dis?" Snuk asked pissed.

"A nigga named Chris and Mohammad." I told Snuk everything that had happened.

He put peroxide on my wound and wrapped it up in a bandage.

"I want you to go right back down there when the Bo'dens leave and tear that joint up. Make an example out of whoever." Snuk instructed.

"Hold up let me get my pump." Domo said. He ran out the door to his house.

"Joe, I'ma flip that nigga ass like a burger. This his second try." I informed Snuk.

"Fuck that I'm gonna kill this nigga!" Snuk snapped, as he walked toward the door.

I grabbed Snuk arm, "Remember bro what you always tell me...patience." I reminded him. "This is my battle...let me fight it."

Snuk just stared at me, he reached in his waist band and pulled out his 10mm Glock. "Take this." He handed me the gun.

Domo had come back, the smoke was clear, so me and Domo crept back down 49th Place through the back streets. As we entered the back of the building.

Nobody was out there; the place was a ghost town. We stood still then suddenly Chris came out of the building walking towards a grey Ford Taurus.

I pointed my finger to my lip silently, then pointed towards Chris. He was walking mighty sober to me. I waited until he got in his car, so we could trap him in there.

Chris opened the door, sat in the front seat, and cut the overhead light on. He was looking down at something, before he had a chance Domo walked in front of the car with the 12-gauge double action Mossberg pump.

Chris looked up and knew to say a prayer. Domo cocked the pump and pulled the trigga.

The blast was deafening, Chris's entire chest collapsed from the blast. I calmly walked up to the driver's side window and emptied the entire 10mm clip in his face and head.

I wanted to send a message to Mohammad. No holds barred. Me and Domo broke into a sprint through the back streets after the murder.

"I bet that nigga have a closed casket." I told Domo as we ran back to my house.

"I bet he will too." Domo agreed with a smirk.

CHAPTER TWENTY-SEVEN

The beef was definitely cooking between Mohammad and me. I started punishing Mohammad's men like flies. All was fair in war because there definitely wasn't no love.

I had to flush Mohammad out because I could see that he was a thinker. He played chest well but sat down at the table with the wrong playa this time. One thing about Mohammad he loved to gamble. He had a vicious passion for those dice. It was a big dice game that Snuk had set-up and left. The players didn't know what was going to happen.

We were just wishing upon a star that if Mohammad was in the vicinity he'd show up. Snuk waited for about an hour. Mohammad still didn't show up, so Snuk left. He had to go check on his daughter.

The game was in 49th Street alley. The same alley where Mohammad first shot at me in. I never went down there after that I stayed up Lincoln Heights and hustled.

Snuk said that Mohammad didn't show up, so it wasn't no use in me creeping down there.

"Hey youngin' you workin' wit' some 'em?" A pipe head asked as I stood in my building hallway. It was Fast Mike.

"Yeah, what's up Fast Mike?" I greeted him.

"Shit just out'chere tryna make a dolla. I'm tryna get my lungs out da street." Fast Mike said as he handed me a twenty-dollar bill.

I handed Fast Mike a big boulder rock.

"Oh...oh...Fast Mike 'preciate this youngin'." He said as he zeroed in on the size of the piece of crack I gave him.

"Damn Fast Mike, you still pushing Benny Hills huh?"

"Oh yeah, you kno' my Benny Hills comfortable." He said grinning goofily. His penny loafers were leaning like the Eiffel Tower.

"Hey Fast Mike, I still got ya baby on some brand-new slippers, a'ight." I told him.

"Alrighty den, I'ma be waiting too." Fast Mike said as he sped off to smoke his crack.

It was getting dark outside when another pipe head walked up.

"What's up mama?" I asked the pipe head. A caramel colored lady.

"Heey…baby boy. Shoot me some' em for forty dollas." She said.

"Gotcha." I agreed as I reached in my pocket to bless her.

I'm surprise you not down there gambling. You up here by yourself getting all the money. I see while all the other boys is down there losing theirs." She said.

"Nah, I'm 'bout this money." I said as I put my hand out for the money.

"Ya know everybody down there…Snoop, West, John…Mohammad…Ralph…"

"Hold up, did you say Mohammad?" I asked now interested.

"Yeah, he down there sitting down, I just left him." She confirmed.

My heart skipped a beat, I was so exhilarated. I handed her three bags of crack. She hurried up and closed her hand thinking, I dropped three in her hand by mistake. I smirked, she rushed off thinking she came up.

I was just blessing her dumb ass. I rushed in the house and changed clothes. I put on all black from head to toe and grabbed my Glock .40 with an extended clip. I was so excited, I was shaking. I crept down to the alley from the back way.

I scanned the scene and to my amazement niggas was still gambling. These niggas could do this all day because their money was long. That's when I saw him bent down on his knees observing the shooter shoot the dice.

As I walked up to the dice game, a dark-skinned dude asked me did I want to bet. He had a fist full of hundred-dollar bills. I told him I was straight.

"Cuz you gonna bet some 'em?" another dude asked me as I approached the crap game smoothly.

"Nah lova. I just came to pay my dues." I told him.

He turned his focus back on the dice game. Everybody was focused on the game.

I pulled out my bandanna and tied it around my neck. I eased my way over to Mohammad, he was oblivious to my presence. As Mohammad turned his head I reached up under my shirt, grabbed the 40 caliber, and pointed it at Mohammad's head.

The crowd of dudes at the dice game slowly left their money and backed away.

Most dudes turned their heads because they didn't want to be a witness to no homicide.

Mohammad realized what was happening as he turned. I heard him gasp surprised, but it was too late. I looked him directly in his eyes and calmly pulled the trigga. The Glock exploded with a thunderous roar.

The sound broke the crowd's trance and niggas dispersed in every direction running. Mohammad fell back, I calmly walked over to him and shot him nine times in the head and face, disfiguring his melon. Blood was soaking the pavement with clots of thick blood.

The fresh smell of hot piss and copper arose from his dead body. I saw a tear fall from one good eye, even in death you can cry, but you'll still die, there'll be no tears in the end.

Word had traveled that I had murdered Mohammad in cold blood. I'd finally gotten my revenge, Snuk panicked.

"Squirrel, what the fuck did you do man?" He fussed.

"I smashed that nigga ass!" I started rapping a tune. "Ain't no love for an enemy, he's no friend of me and when I catch him…I'ma lay 'em in da streets." I rapped.

"Nigga dis ain't no fuckin' time for jokin' Squirrel." Snuk yelled.

"Man, what you trippin' off, Joe…you knew he had dat coming. I let that hamma nail his head to the ground. Snuk you on some other shit!" I said.

"Nah, I ain't trippin' stupid…the muthafuckin' homicide been round this joint questioning muthafuckas wit' yo' name in their mouths. That's the other shit I'm on since I got to be trippin." Snuk said angrily.

Hearing that definitely wiped the smile off my face.

"Now your beef gonna be wit' the justice system. With a jury of twelve and believe me that system…innocent or guilty…we're all guilty no matter what the circumstances. They don't give a fuck about who killed your dog or who shot you, or that you grew up in the ghetto, fatherless, mother on drugs, whatever. All they see is a black young man, who's a drug dealer, and a killer. They win either way. You kill a dude you go to prison for life. You get a coward ass codefendant, he snitch on you, but they still give him a hand full of time. It's a no-win situation, them judges motto is to kill two birds with one stone." Snuk educated.

"Fuck it, I'ma kill all my witnesses 'fore they get me. These muthafuckas gonna have to prove dis shit." I said in defiance.

"Shorty it's not that easy, just admit it you finally did a sloppy job. Remember what I always say…patience. You got cocky Squirrel…damnit!"

I knew I had to leave the city. Homicide ran in Big Doris's house looking for me.

They had flyers out with my photo on them, I tried to remember every face that was out there the night of the murder. I was gonna try to down everyone, but I couldn't remember.

I boarded the Greyhound bus and traveled to a cousin's crib in New York on 175th Street in The Bronx. I called my cousin from the Greyhound bus station and she came to pick me up. Her name was Sharise.

Sharise was light-skinned with pretty, brown eyes and a body, Janet Jackson would die for.

She was a distant cousin who I hadn't seen in many years. I told her I wanted to visit for a while. She didn't know I was wanted for murder in D.C.

I took ten thousand dollars with me, Sharise drove down Madison Avenue to a little apartment complex hidden amongst some houses. I liked the location, my stay in New York was very fun. I was balling and Sharise and her girlfriend was loving it. Sharise was heterosexual turned lesbian.

She had a son from her previous relationship, he was six years old. New York was fun, but when the money ran low, so did the fun. Sharise was getting moody all of a sudden.

I noticed her change of attitude one night coming back from Coney Island in Brooklyn New York. We went there and had a good time, but on our way back Sharise became snappy.

She got to complaining about me using her telephone too much, eating all the fruity Pebbles, and more. I was supplying most of the food, weed, and outings, so I had to wonder what the problem really was.

At that moment I felt out of place so, I knew I had to leave New York. The next morning I packed all the clothes I brought up there and asked Sharise for a ride to the bus station. She pretended to be sadden by my decision to depart. But I felt as though she was happy.

Once we arrived at the Greyhound bus station I said my goodbyes and she left.

"See ya bitch." I mumbled under my breath.

I had enough money left for a one-way ticket to D.C. I arrived back in Washington D.C. home sweet home. I went to my aunt Tinan's house.

I knew I couldn't stay long, but I needed a place to lay my head low for the time being. The rest of my money was stashed in Big Doris's crib, I needed that.

I crept back around Lincoln Heights and it was as if I was an instant celebrity. Everybody greeted me with so much love. I'd only been gone for four months.

"Damn Squirrel…what's up young?" Tye said excited walking up, embracing me with a big hug.

"Look at my nigga." Greg said.

"Damn young you fly as shit." Ronald said.

I had on a green and white Nautica sweat suit, with a pair of green and white low-cut Air Force Ones, and a yellow and green bandanna wrapped around my head.

Everywhere I went there was love being shown. It felt good to be welcomed back to the hood. My man Stutterin' Dirk who had the candy apply blue Nissan 300 ZX and the big-headed Pitbull named Shocker, gave me the latest run down on the hood politics, murders, and hustle game.

Before I knew it I was back hustling in the hood. Snuk had my car, so I drove around in Dirk's Z, plus I wasn't gonna drive my own shit.

Two weeks had pass since I returned to D.C. I was living as if nothing ever happened, police wasn't beeming a nigga, so I felt relaxed. I thought about Keisha and decided to pay her a visit. I hadn't seen her in months, I missed my baby.

I hopped in the car and drove up Ridge Road. I parked, got out, and walked to Keisha's apartment building. I knocked on the door.

"Who is it?" Keisha's lovely voice hollered.

"Me." I replied.

"Who is me?" She asked opening the door.

"Ooh my Gawd!" Keisha screamed, covering her eyes. Then she ran and jumped into my arms, hugging me.

"Boy where the hell you been…I been looking all over for you. At least you could have called a bitch…even if it was just to say fuck you…I'm a'ight."

"I just had to get away and find myself." I told her.

Keisha hit me on the shoulder. "Boy don't play wit' me."

"Seriously though I had to get away." I repeated.

Keisha walked into the apartment and I followed behind her. As I walked in the apartment.

I looked to my right to find a dude sitting on the couch, with his right foot resting on the coffee table I bought, with my favorite pillow, I bought for Keisha, resting under his arm. He looked comfortable as hell, he was dark-skinned, medium built, handsome with a grimace on his face.

Keisha walked in the back room right past this nigga.

Who da fuck is dis?' I thought.

"What's up lova?" I spoke.

"What's up…" he paused then asked the magic words. "Who you?"

"Funny you asked, 'cause I was gonna ask you the same question." I told him.

"Hmmp." He smirked sarcastically. "My name Melvin from 34th Street southeast.

I didn't give a fuck where he was from. This nigga had his foot up on the table I'd paid for and was squeezing my favorite pillow. That ticked me off.

I stepped off in the back room to check Keisha about her company.

"Man, who the fuck is that nigga in the living room with his foot on the coffee table and caressing the pillow I bought you?" I mumbled angrily.

"Oh, he should know what time it is. Yeah Fox that's my friend I met him when you pulled ya disappearin' act." She replied.

I couldn't be mad because she kept it real. I was about to leave, Keisha grabbed my arm.

"Where you think you going Mister? Boy I wish you would try to leave when I haven't seen yo' ass in months." She threatened.

"Dig Keisha I ain't gonna disrespect your boyfriend." I said. My heart was crushed for real.

"Nigga I didn't say that was my boyfriend. Listen…I said friend, I told him all about you. So, he knows where my heart at. It's with you Fox."

I stared into Keisha's big pretty green eyes. I knew she was telling the truth.

As I walked back into the living room the dude Melvin was at the coffee table pretending to clean a .380 caliber hand gun. When I entered the living room he acted like he didn't even notice me. He kept turning the gun this way, that way, wiping it down with a white cloth.

I recognized his intimidation tactic, but this dude really didn't know what he was getting himself into. He continued cleaning his gun and acting like I wasn't there.

"Uh huh." I cleared my throat loudly.

When he looked up I was handing him a massive sick looking, all black Mac-10 .45 caliber with a thirty shot extended clip.

"Could you clean this while you at it?" I asked.

His mouth dropped as he just stared at the mini machine gun.

"Oh…ah…nah…I…I can't clean…I mean…" He couldn't even get the words out.

"Well put that shit up and play wit' it at yo' house." I said.

Keisha was standing behind me fingering her left ear with her head titled to one side.

"Ah Melvin this is my heart…Fox. That I told you about!" She said.

The dude Melvin looked as if he'd seen a ghost. He tried to say something, but the fear wouldn't allow his mouth to form any words.

"I…I…I…h…heard about him." Melvin stuttered. "Keisha I…I… love you how could you do this to me?" H damn near cried.

"Melvin I been told you when we first started kicking it that I had a man. We were going through some problems, but whenever he came back you gonna have to respect him and leave."

Melvin started pouting.

"This shit ridiculous." I mumbled under my breath.

"But…but…but…Keisha!" He said.

"It ain't no muthafuckin' ifs, ands, or buts. I been told you not to catch feelings because I got a nigga, I love." Keisha said her anger rising.

I kept my eye trained on him because this joker had a hamma in his hand and I knew shit could turn haywire. I clicked the safety off the Mac-10.

I wasn't going to tell slim to leave, because that was Keisha's company. As bad as I wanted to intervene, I didn't I kept my mouth shut and my gun ready.

"Keisha…I got feel…" he was cut off by Keisha.

"Nigga you actin' like a real bitch…get the fuck outta my house!" Keisha screamed. "Now!"

Melvin looked at me, then her, then he quickly glanced at the gruesome looking gun in my hand. He decided otherwise, he put the gun in his pocket, got up, and left.

The front door slammed as he descended the steps. I watched him go outside, get in his car, and drive off angrily.

I let out a slow breath and put my gun up. Keisha grabbed my hand and pulled me into the backroom. She kissed me passionately as she peeled my clothes off. She slowly undressed and got in the bed, Keisha grabbed my dick and put it in her vagina, she rode me hard.

I grabbed her small waist as I pumped in and out of her. Keisha cried out as she came. I laid Keisha on her back and put her right leg over my shoulder as I entered her.

She gasped as I pushed the full length deep down into her warmth. I began to hump furiously.

Keisha wrapped her arms around my neck, moaning.

"Baby...baby...I love you. Tell me...that you never gonna leave me again. Tell me..." Keisha said out of breath as I pumped away in and out of her.

"I won't leave you baby...I won't." I groaned as I bent down and passionately kissed her.

We made love all night. The next morning, I woke up with Keisha in my arms. I kissed her forehead, she looked up at me with those beautiful green eyes.

"Fox, fuck all this shit...let's get together...get our own place...move away." She said.

"I've been thinking the same thing." I told her.

"We can do this on our own...I love you...let's stop bickering amongst each other." She said.

"I feel you!" I agreed.

"Nah seriously Fox stay with me...don't leave no more...my father left me when I was young...I don't want you leaving me too!" She begged.

"Baby I'm serious...I ain't gonna leave you...girl I love your ass." I said as I kissed her on her lips. "I've missed you too." I said.

"I've missed you, too!" Keisha said as she kissed me.

I got up out of the bed, took a shower, then put my clothes on.

"Baby where you going?" Keisha asked.

"I'm going to pick up the rest of this money from around the Heights. I'll be back."

"Boo fuck dat money...stay here wit' me." Keisha pleaded. "You just got here Fox...damn spend some time wit' me."

I walked over to Keisha and kissed her.

"Baby I'ma..." she cut me off.

"Fox don't go." Keisha whined.

"Look I promise to be right back. I'm just going to pick this money up. I'm coming with you. I decided that last night baby. I'm through wit' dis shit." I said as I looked in Keisha's eyes.

Keisha pouted, she still didn't want me to go. Keisha got up put some booty shorts and a T-shirt on and walked me to the front door. I gave her a long passionate kiss. I'll be back to tap dat ass." I said, pinching her ass.

Keisha squeaked with laughter, "I love you Jonathan Fox." She said as I was leaving.

"I love you more Keisha." I said as I exited the building.

I arrived around Lincoln Heights. I posted up and kicked it with a few homies. Today was a good day, money was coming and it was just a vibrant day. I decided to walk around the basketball court to see what was happening. A lot of females was outside gawking watching dudes play basketball. I posted up at the fence and kicked it with the homie Ramon.

As we kicked it, I was watching the streets. I saw a police car past, I paid no attention to it. About twenty minutes later a helicopter was flying over us pretty low. I decided to leave as I turned around, I heard...

"Freeze...get your hands in the air!" An F.B.I agent screamed at me while pointing a fully loaded automatic M-16 Rifle at me.

The agents rushed out in every direction. I was surrounded, and the helicopter hovered over my head. I wanted to pull my gun out and make them kill me. Through the throng of F.B.I. agents, two detectives emerged from the crowd.

"Well...well...well...Mr. Jonathan Fox...we finally meet...again. I believe we were formally introduced a while ago." The other detective said.

"I thought we'd visiting you in the morgue...instead of putting somebody else's ass in the morgue." His partner told the detective.

It was the two detectives from the hospital when I got shot.

"My name is detective Collins." The short brown-skinned black smart mouth one said.

"And my name is detective Dalilah." The other said.

Dalilah was a tall medium, build white cop, "And today we'll be your escorts." Detective Collins said sarcastically.

"We know you have a gun on you. So I'ma walk over to you, retrieve the gun, and you'll never hear about it again. Unless it's the murder weapon, but I'm sure it's not. You are well trained at this." Detective Dalilah said.

I held my hands up as the detective walked over, took my gun, winked his eye, and put it in his front coat pocket.

"Take 'em boys!" He hollered.

The agents rushed in, handcuffed me, and put me in the back of a police squad car. I saw the detectives and agents shaking hands. I looked at the sad faces of people watching me. Dudes walked around with their heads down.

"Nooo...Fox!" A voice wailed at a distance.

I looked and saw Tye holding Keisha. She was crying hysterically.

"Nooo...baby...no. I told you to stay with me!" She cried out as Tye held her back from running through the crowd of police.

I leaned my head back as Keisha's words replayed in my mind.

"Don't go baby...stay here wit' me...we can move away!" A tear fell down my face.

The two detectives sat in the car and drove off. Before they tried to make small conversation.

"I plead the fifth. I ain't saying nothin' till I see my lawyer." I told them.

"Fine wit' us, but you're gonna need help because your ass will never see these streets again...so get one last good long look son!" Detective Collins said.

"We been heard about your murderous spree, but we ain't have enough evidence. Woo-wee, now ya finally fucked up boy! This one gonna stick like glue!" Detective Collins said a little too excited.

"Man fuck you." I yelled.

"Well, that's what the judge gonna do to you."

I put my head back and closed my eyes. In my tender life I tried, the streets made me a monster. I'ma miss them...I'ma miss them.

'It's so hard to say goodbye to yesterday'!

EPILOGUE

I laid in a four-corner dingy cell in D.C. jail. The cell had a foul odor that reeked of piss and shit. I couldn't get comfortable, so I cleaned and scrubbed the cell from the ceiling to the floor.

I was extradited from Oak Hill juvenile detention to D.C. jail. I was housed in the notorious block called the juvenile block. This is where all the most violent dangerous juveniles were housed, after being title sixteen from the D.C. superior courts.

Title sixteen is when a juvenile is charged as an adult for the nature and severity of the offense he is charged with.

"Trays...trays...chowtime! Hold it down!" The big belly C.O. yelled.

I took the Styrofoam tray and cup to my bunk, then looked inside to find what we called river rat and shit on the shingle. I didn't know what the food was just some chopped meat, chopped up with gravy.

I was fresh from the bricks, I couldn't eat that shit. I sat that tray on my bars.

"Hey slim," a voice from the next cell called over. "You gonna eat dat?" He asked.

This had to be a greedy nigga.

"Nah, young." I said as I handed him the tray. I went back and pressed my bunk.

A commotion broke out. "Hey C.O...C.O." Another juvenile called out. "I need to see you where my tray?"

"You didn't get a tray." The C.O. asked.

"Nah Joe." He said.

"Well youngin your tray must have been called." The C.O. said walking off.

"Muhfucka ain't no nigga taking nothin' from he." He yelled after the C.O. "You stupid fat bitch, but I got that ass nigga…believe that!" The angry Juvenile yelled after the C.O.

The other juveniles banged as well, hyping the angry juvenile up. He went to the back of his room and returned to the bars with two peanut jars and a big shampoo bottle filled with feces, spoiled milk, and piss. He was about to get busy.

"Hey youngin' man just chill Joe." A sensible voice from another juvenile tried to reason with him." That shit ain't worth it."

"Nah fuck that young…don't no nigga carry me like a bitch." He insisted. "For real ain't going for nothing."

He was going to shit the C.O. down throwing the contents on him from the jars. He imagined the C.O.s face when he executed his plan. The mere thought brought him pure satisfaction, well worth any consequence.

"Hey young!" the juvenile called over to his friend beside him. "Get that C.O. up here for me."

The other Juvenile anxiously agreed, wanting to see the drama unfold. "Hey, C.O…hey C.O.!" *Boom…boom…boom…* "Hey C.O.!" The other juvenile yelled and kicked. "My toilet!"

"Yeah…yeah…yeah shut that shit up!" The big belly C.O. yelled out as he walked down the tier towards the cell.

When the C.O. reached the juveniles door. A hand brought the peanut butter jars through the bars and caught the C.O. dead in his face.

"Aarrgghh…" the C.O. screamed in disbelief realizing that he'd been set-up.

Then he started spraying the C.O. with the shampoo bottle full of raw feces, spoiled milk, and piss.

"Yeah muhfucka call this out…bitch ass nigga!" The juvenile taunted with glee.

The smell was sickening. I covered my nose and mouth with my shirt. The smell lite up the entire tier. All the juvenile inmates erupted in taunts and curses as the C.O. stumbled not sure to wipe his face or what. Another C.O. witnessed the assault and ran upstairs to his assistance, escorting him to the nearest mop closet, to wash off.

The tier continued to cheer and curse at the C.O. until he was gone. The noise started to subside because the juveniles knew this wasn't over yet. Everybody started flooding their toilets preparing for war.

"Hey Roy, you a'ight Joe?" A juvenile hollered.

"Yeah." Roy replied. "I shitted that bitch ass nigga down good."

"Yeah young you got slim sweet." Said another juvy.

"You know dey comin'." Said another voice. "Be strong cuz they gonna try to crush you. You know, that right?"

"Always cuz always." Said Roy.

They all saw the five big officers return headed by the man who we named Big Sergeant. We knew what time it was, you could see the smirk on his face. This was the part of his job, he lived for.

"Roy!" A voice exclaimed once more. "Rumble them muthafuckas."

"I ain't ducking no drama...bring it!" Roy yelled trying to pump himself up for the ass whupping that was coming.

"Y'all need five muhfuckas for one man!" One juvy screamed out.

"Y'all some cowards." Another yelled.

"Give him a fair one on one." Another yelled.

"Shut up or you're next." Barked Big Sergeant.

"Suck my dick!" Another juvenile screamed out.

They walked to Roy's cell door.

"Inmate Filton lay down on the floor and place your hands behind your head." Big Sergeant ordered.

"Fuck you!" Roy screamed.

"This is your final warning. Inmate Filton lay down or…He's got a weapon!" Big Sergeant screamed.

Roy sprayed more feces from his shit bottle in defiance.

"Take this bitches." Roy blurted.

I heard the cell door open and the officers rushed in. water flowed in my cell from the flooding. Roy was the average size sixteen-year-old. But he put up one helluva fight.

"Fuck y'all cowards… the man down!" I yelled, wishing I could get out of my cell and help him. I didn't know him, but I knew who the enemy was, and we had to show some camaraderie.

After the officers carried Roy out of the cell 'ass naked' they rushed him to the hole in South-1.

Everybody was banging, hollering, cursing, making noises. It was complete pandemonium, it was definitely another world inside here.

****

Two weeks later…

"Fox you have a visit!!" The female C.O. Ms. Jackson hollered.

"Who da fuck could this be?" I asked under my breath.

I put my all blue jail jumpsuit on with my black wave cap and Timberland boots. I was fresh compared to jail standards.

The officer put the handcuffs on me, then escorted me to the visiting hall.

I entered the noisy visiting room, had the cuffs removed, then walked towards the visiting booth.

Out of all the niggas that were my so-called friends none of them came to visit me, but here sitting in front of me was my man, since I first moved around Lincoln Heights…Black Mike. I was heartfelt, he smiled as I grabbed the receiver.

"What's up young?" He greeted. "You doin' ya push ups I see." He commented.

"Yeah a little some 'em…some 'em. What's up Joe? I'm happy to see you my nigga!" I told him.

"Same here Squirrel." He replied. "The hood ain't the same without you Squirrel. We used to have so much fun when you were home." Black Mike complimented looking sad.

"Hold that head up soldier…ya boy Squirrel gonna be a'ight. I'ma Lincoln Heights Nigga!" I said trying to make Black Mike smile again.

We held a good conversation, until it was time to go.

"Hey Black Mike!"

"Yeah Young!"

"Remember Fast Mike the pipe head?" I asked.

"Yeah…tell me he snitching so I can open his melon." Black Mike offered.

"Nah, Young he not snitchin', we don't know who telling yet. But do me a favor." I told Mike. "I promised to buy Fast Mike a pair of loafers because you know he be rocking his Benny heels, penny loafers.

Black Mike busted out laughing. "Yeah Joe, them joints leaning like a 64' Impala."

"Take him down Georgetown and buy him an expensive pair of Fergamos or Stacy Adams loafers. Make sure he picks them out and tell him that's from me…and that I kept my promise."

"Last call…time to go Fox!" An officer yelled.

I got up and put my fist to the glass. Mike got up and held his fist to the glass where mine was at. His eyes started to tear up.

"I got a court date tomorrow, wish me luck nigga." I told him.

"I got you young...I got you." He said.

The C.O. handcuffed me, as he was taking me out of the visiting booth.

Mike just stood there and stared at the officer escorting me away. I turned around and bang my fist against my chest, then nodded my head, silently letting Black Mike know I was gonna hold it down. Black Mike nodded then walked away.

I was in the courtroom and I had found out that the main government witness was Hairio bitch ass. I knew I should had killed him that day the jump outs chased me through the woods. And I found him sitting on his car. This was the same nigga mugging and selling me death.

What part of the game was this shit. I had just come out of the Bull pen, where some dudes had just beaten the dog shit out of another dude.

When I entered the court room. I had to sit and wait for the fucking judge to return from his chamber. As I was waiting, I saw a white female speaking to another woman in a suit they both looked over at me then the white woman began to walk forward in my direction.

As she got closer, she had a resemblance to someone I knew.

"Oh, you don't remember me huh...Mr...um...Fox?" She smiled a beautiful smile with perfect teeth.

I remembered her then, it was the white woman that drove the 535i BMW on Division Avenue who I sold the dope to. Megan was her name.

"Yes, it's me Mr...never answered my call." She said. "I never told you my profession, yes I am a lawyer and I decided to handle your case pro bono.

I've heard all about you mister. But I can't get you completely off because there is too much evidence against you. Two eye witnesses, especially this guy Hairio…he could be a prosecutor himself the way he described you to the grand jury. Baby you in good hands though." She said, patting my hand, then walked away.

Four months later I arrived in court again for my sentencing…

"Mr. Fox, I don't care if you're a juvenile, do you understand the charges against you?" The judge asked.

"Yes, your honor I do." I responded.

"You killed a man in cold blood…do you have anything to say on your behalf Mr. Fox?"

"Yeah, my life wasn't perfect. I hope one day I'll be able to embrace society again and teach the youths that this life ain't the way."

"We'll be accepting the plea Ms. Richards brought forth. If it wasn't for that you would've received life. Instead you are being sentenced to fifteen to thirty years. You'll be able to see the parole board in fifteen years. I pray that you use that time wisely." The judge said.

"Yes, sir your honor." I replied.

The courtroom was in murmurs. I hugged my lawyer Megan and thanked her. The two detectives were fuming with anger as I walked by. They wanted me to get life. Detective Collins pointed his finger in a gun motion at me.

Detective Dalilah just shook his head in disbelief. Yeah instead of a natural life sentence, my lawyer had me cop to second degree murder. I was sentenced to fifteen to life. Fifteen years is still a very long time. I got up and everything around me slowed to a crawl as I walked away to be taken to prison in slow motion.

They'll be singing in dark times…ah yes singing about the dark times!'

Made in the USA
Middletown, DE
10 July 2021